the
Triumph of Eve
& Other Subversive Bible Tales

the
Triumph of Eve
& Other Subversive Bible Tales

Matt Biers-Ariel

Walking Together, Finding the Way
SKYLIGHT PATHS Publishing
Woodstock, Vermont

The Triumph of Eve & Other Subversive Bible Tales

2004 First Printing
©2004 by Matt Biers-Ariel

For information regarding permission to reprint material from this book, please write or fax your request to SkyLight Paths Publishing, Permissions Department, at the address / fax number listed below, or e-mail your request to permissions@ skylightpaths.com.

Library of Congress Cataloging-in-Publication Data
Biers-Ariel, Matt.
The triumph of Eve & other subversive Bible tales / Matt Biers-Ariel.
    p. cm.
ISBN 1-59473-040-7 (hardcover)
1. Bible stories, English. I. Title: Triumph of Eve and other subversive Bible tales. II. Title.
BS550.3.B54 2004
220.9'505—dc22

2004008691

10   9   8   7   6   5   4   3   2   1
Manufactured in Canada
Jacket design and illustration: Sara Dismukes

> SkyLight Paths is creating a place where people of different spiritual traditions come together for challenge and inspiration, a place where we can help each other understand the mystery that lies at the heart of our existence.
>
> SkyLight Paths sees both believers and seekers as a community that increas-ingly transcends traditional boundaries of religion and denomination— people wanting to learn from each other, *walking together, finding the way.*

SkyLight Paths, "Walking Together, Finding the Way" and colophon are trademarks of LongHill Partners, Inc., registered in the U.S. Patent and Trademark Office.

Walking Together, Finding the Way
Published by SkyLight Paths Publishing
A Division of LongHill Partners, Inc.
Sunset Farm Offices, Route 4, P.O. Box 237
Woodstock, VT 05091
Tel: (802) 457-4000   Fax: (802) 457-4004
www.skylightpaths.com

to Yonah and Solomon
may you always wrestle with God
and
to Djina, my other half

Contents

Foreword

A few months ago, God and I were enjoying a pleasant evening in the Milky Way playing with Orion's two dogs, Canis Major and Canis Minor.

"You know, lately I've been thinking a lot about My Bible," said God, throwing a red dwarf star for the dogs to fetch. "Excellent stories. First-rate commandments. And without a doubt, it's Earth's best seller of all time."

I didn't want to ruin another perfectly good evening bickering over religion, so I said, "How hot are those red dwarfs anyway? Think the dogs could get burned?"

God sighed. "Only one problem: A lot of humans just don't get it."

"A lot of humans just don't get anything," I replied. "They're denser than black holes."

Canis Major returned with the star in its mouth, but before the canine could drop it for another throw, Minor jumped up to grab it out of the larger dog's mouth. Major held on, and both dogs tugged until the star exploded into a supernova.

I donned my sunglasses and God spoke. "Remember when We thought We could get rid of evil with a good, long flood?"

"Sorry," I said, "that was Your brainstorm."

God chuckled. "You wouldn't have taken any credit for it if it worked?"

I absentmindedly played with a bit of cosmic dust and compressed it into an asteroid.

"But," continued God, "that's not My point. My point is that when most humans read about the Flood, they see a happy children's story that ends with a dove flying over a rainbow. They miss the deeper meanings."

God touched me on the shoulder. "The people need help."

"The only thing that could possibly help that species would be a big, fat meteor," I muttered to myself.

God looked deeply into my eyes and said, "They need help getting to the essence of the Bible. They need help seeing the essential questions that the Bible poses, questions that I want them to wrestle with."

Pregnant pause.

"So, Gabriella, My precious angel."

I winced and mumbled, "Here it comes."

"I want you to go down to Earth and find a guy named Matt. You'll find him in North America. Can't miss him. He's got curly black hair and wears glasses."

"No problem," I said. "Only 57,493 fit that description."

"Look for a bike," God said. "He rides one."

"Down to 11,498."

"When you find him," continued God, "explain the Bible fully, and have him write it down in a book."

I stood with my mouth agape. "*Explain the whole Bible to a human?* Hello, God, these creatures are not the brightest stars in the sky. I'll be there forever, and, in case You don't remember, I get rashes when I'm around them too much."

"Who said the whole thing? Just a dozen stories. It'll be easy. The guy's a regular Einstein."

"Right."

"You'll do a terrific job. As always. All right?"

"As if I had a choice."

God smiled. "That's My angel. Listen. Castor and Pollux invited Me for a late-night snack. Gotta run."

God hopped on a nearby comet and zoomed off.

"Good luck!" God called back before disappearing into another galaxy.

"Good luck," I repeated. "Right."

I sighed. There was nothing for me to do but find this guy. When I did, I tried to teach him some Bible. But it was just as I knew it would be. First, I'd tell him a story, and then he'd leave out the most important part. So we had to start all over. This time he'd have the important part, but mix up the characters. So we'd start again. He might have been an Einstein, but Al got the brains in that family.

At last, story after excruciating story, he finally got what I was trying to teach him; at least I think he did. By this time, my rash was breaking out, so I hightailed it out of there before proofing his final draft.

Needless to say, any errors in the stories that follow are this guy's, and this guy's alone. I take no responsibility and wash my hands of this whole wretched project.

Gabriella, Chief Angel
A galaxy far, far from Earth

Preface

There is good reason the Bible is the best-selling book of all time. Whether one sees the Bible as the literal word of God, as a human invention inspired by God, or simply as a piece of ancient literature, it is clear that this book, more than any other, has shaped Western culture and religion into what it is today. Millions of people seek moral guidance in the Bible's pages on a daily or weekly basis. Literature and film have freely borrowed from it. In fact, any person wholly unfamiliar with biblical allusions would be considered a—well, a philistine. Further, it has been argued that the Bible provides the bedrock on which most modern legal systems stand. One last telling influence of this book is that today, some 2,500 years after it was written, parents still go to it when they look for children's names. While Joseph, Jacob, Sarah, and Hannah are perennial favorites, one would be hard-pressed to find a pair of brothers named Cain and Abel.

Despite the Bible's popularity and influence, biblical stories and their meanings are often unclear. After all, many of the words and idioms of the original Hebrew are unfamiliar to us. Even more important than the problems of language, the text itself is filled with ambiguity. The Bible is succinct. Much is left unsaid. For example, the patriarch Abraham is introduced to the reader when he is already seventy-five years old. The Bible tells us absolutely nothing about this central figure's prior life.

Unlike the U.S. Constitution, the author(s) of the Bible left no notes or letters for us to pore over in order to discover original intent. So for generations, people have created stories to try to make sense of this book. In fact, some of the most famous "biblical" stories are these interpretations, such as the story about how Abraham discovered monotheism by watching the night sky when he was a young boy.

Paradoxically, the Bible's very ambiguity imbues it with more power, rather than less. Since there can be no single interpretation of the Bible, its multiple meanings allow each story to speak to each individual reader. The concept of multiple meanings is not new. Traditional Judaism claims that each word of the Torah, the first five books of the Bible, contains *seventy* meanings.

Unfortunately, many of us have been taught a one-dimensional Bible. For example, the story of Adam and Eve conveys the penalty for the sin of disobedience while explaining why man dominates woman. Abraham is the story of how one man's faith launched Western religion. Beware of jealousy is the lesson of Cain and Abel.

The Triumph of Eve and Other Subversive Bible Tales is a collection of stories—some whimsical, some serious—that start from a close reading of the original text and its commentaries. Sometimes they attempt to resolve the ambiguity of the Bible. Sometimes they try to shed light on a part of a story that is often overlooked. Either way, these stories challenge several of the monolithic understandings and teachings of the Bible. They ask the reader to grapple with questions and insights that are often hidden in the original text. Examples of questions raised include:

- Can the tension between justice and mercy be resolved?

- How can knowledge of one's death be life-affirming?

- What makes someone become a suicide bomber?

- Why does a physical disability often bring strength?

- What is the essential nature of the human being?

Each story in this collection raises questions like these. Some stories even offer answers. Are they the right answers? That is for you to decide. My hope is that *The Triumph of Eve* gives you food for thought, ideas to ruminate over. If you can digest particular ideas without suffering indigestion, terrific. If you spit them out in favor of others, great. The important thing is for you to become engaged with the Bible as generations have done for over 2,500 years. If *The Triumph of Eve* helps you do this, that will be enough.

The Triumph
of Eve

O y," said God. "Such a week."

And such a week it was. It began when God came upon a primordial ooze in the far reaches of the Milky Way Galaxy. To this chaos, God added light, separated water from land, planted plants, and transformed the mess into a respectable planet. Next, God filled the sky with birds, the water with fish, and the land with creatures. God stepped back, beheld the finished creation, and proclaimed, "Not bad."

God eased into a well-deserved bath, when an out-of-breath angel flew in and announced, "The precipitation runoff from the Himalayan region has created an inundation preventing the big-eared pachyderm from reaching her preferred nutrient source!"

"Big-eared pachyderm?" said God, raising an eyebrow. "Elephant?"

"She can't get to her peanuts because the river is too high to cross."

"So much for My soak," God sighed and gingerly stepped out of the tub.

While God toweled dry, dozens of angels flew in with more bad news about that new planet, Earth.

"Maybe six days was too rushed," murmured the Creator.

God was in no mood to repair the planet, but what were the options? Suddenly, a lightning bolt flashed above God's head—appoint one of the animals to fix the mess.

1

The question was: Whom to employ?

"Bear? Brave, yes, but such a klutz. Always getting his head stuck in the honey. I'd go hoarse yelling at him all the time. What about Ant? Now there's a worker for you. But smart as a block of wood. How about Owl? That one's sharp. But her hours. Oy. With all that night hooting, I'd never get any peace."

God went through all the animals and realized that not a single one was right for the job. A new animal needed to be created. One that would be more—well, Godlike. The new animal needed to be coordinated, intelligent, and diurnal. God gathered different-colored clays from around the globe, mixed them together, and formed a new creature. God blew spirit into the creature's nostrils, and Human began to breathe.

Gabriella, God's chief angel, flew down from a nearby cloud and was about to add the final touch, wisdom, when God grabbed her by the halo.

"Hey, whoa there!" God said. "Don't do that."

"No?"

"Wisdom's not something you give. It's something Human earns through experience, pain, reflection, and sacrifice. Give it for free, and Human will despise it."

"But then Human will possess all that power without anything to counterbalance it. Trust me. You're playing with fire."

"So who invented fire?"

"You're the Boss," said Gabriella, and withheld wisdom.

As God turned to leave, a second angel flew in brandishing a thick roll of parchment.

"What's this?" God asked.

"More problems with Your new world."

God whistled. "This job's bigger than I thought. Two hands won't be enough."

So while Human lay on the ground sleeping, God removed

a rib, divided the soul, took a bit more clay, and transformed Human into two creatures, one male and one female.

● ◖▬ ●

"Adam, Eve. Eve, Adam," God said, introducing one to the other after they awoke.

As soon as they were steady on their feet, God strolled Adam and Eve through the Garden of Eden. Rose and jasmine filled the air with their delicate perfumes. Rainbow hues of color glittered through the deep blue sky as butterflies and birds flashed their wings overhead. Adam and Eve stuffed grapes, dates, and figs into their mouths as fast as they could grab them.

"This is great!" Adam exclaimed, wiping grape juice from his chin.

"Glad you like it," said God, "but to tell you the truth, it could use a little fixing up. That's your job."

God produced a contract and a fountain pen. "By the authority vested in Me, I hereby appoint you, Adam and Eve, caretakers of Earth. Sign."

God continued taking Adam and Eve through the garden until they came to a walled-in area. A locked wrought-iron gate led into the enclosure. God placed a key into the padlock and unlocked the gate. They stepped inside and found a single tree. While the rest of Creation looked as new and fresh as its one-week age, this solitary tree was gnarled and stooped. The ancient-looking tree, however, held a few golden fruit that sparkled like the sun. Eve plucked one from the tree and was overcome by a scent sweeter than anything else in the garden. As she cradled the delightful fruit in her hands, she thought she heard it whisper, "Take a bite." As if in a trance, Eve lifted the fruit to her mouth.

God grabbed her arms. "Hey, whoa there! Don't do that! This is the Tree of Knowledge of Good and Evil. Take a bite and you'll die."

Created immortal, Adam and Eve did not understand the word "die."

God explained. "You know that soul I gave you? When you die, I take it back, and your body turns back into earth."

"Into a lump of clay?" said Adam incredulously. "You must be crazy."

Eve inspected the fruit in her hand and asked, "What's Knowledge of Good and Evil?"

Before God could answer, Adam snatched the fruit from Eve, smashed it on the ground, and demanded the key from God.

God handed it to Adam, who walked out the gate. God and Eve followed. Adam locked the gate behind them.

"For my first duty as caretaker, I lock this gate and throw away the key."

Adam threw the key with all his might; it landed miles away, striking Snake on the head.

God thought, "If I didn't want the fruit, I would have locked the gate and tossed the key back inside. Maybe I was too quick about Owl."

Eve, apparently reading God's mind, disagreed and said, "I would have put the key on a chain around my neck."

Adam glared at Eve.

"Well, I mean, we don't even know what this wisdom is," said Eve. "Maybe it's good."

"Yeah, right," Adam replied. "Maybe it's good. Good enough to die for. You must be crazy."

Eve clenched her fist. "Don't call me crazy!"

"Uh, I better be going," said God. God's cumulous chariot instantly appeared. God climbed in and, in an explosion of thunder, was gone.

From the heavens, Adam and Eve heard a faint "Good luck!"

●　◍　◐

Adam and Eve loved the Garden of Eden. Life for them was pleasant. Wake up, eat some berries, take a leisurely stroll, share a banana, lie down for a nap, talk to the animals, take another nap, swim in a river, have dinner, sleep, wake up the next morning, and start all over again.

One day while Eve was speaking with Snake, Snake said, "After many hours of careful field observations, I have deduced that every single animal in our beloved garden has a reason for existence, a purpose, if you will. For example, my hunting expertise keeps the rodent population at bay, preventing them from becoming a nuisance. Bee, without a single word of complaint, tirelessly flies from flower to flower gathering nectar, making honey, and pollinating plants. Condor, by devouring carcasses, decomposes unsightly remains, facilitating the recycling of nutrients.

"Indeed, the only creatures whose reason for being I have been wholly unable to fathom are you and the man. Pardon my inquisitiveness, but what exactly do you do?"

"What do we do? Our job is to care for the garden."

Snake slapped his tail and chortled, "My! What a developed sense of humor you possess, a comic genius."

"What's so funny?"

"Indeed!" laughed Snake, holding his sides. "Examine our surroundings and tell me whether this garden is or is not quite a wreck, perhaps even a calamity. In fact, just last night I was contemplating a correspondence to God to apply for disaster relief."

Eve raised her hand. "You don't need to call God, because we're the caretakers."

"Well, this certainly is news," said Snake. "The humans are the party responsible for garden maintenance."

Suddenly, the wind picked up. Snake and Eve found themselves fending off leaves, twigs, and fruit flying through the air. While Eve pulled a sticky fig from her hair, the ground shook with a loud boom, and the wind ceased as quickly as it had begun. Eve and Snake went to investigate the boom's source and discovered a large, uprooted tree lying across the path.

"So, caretaker, you will remove this vegetation from the thoroughfare?"

"Of course."

"And at what time shall the way be navigable?"

"You mean when?"

"Yes, when? I crawl it every morning to take tea with my reptilian comrades."

Eve examined the tree, scratched her head, made some calculations on her fingers, and answered, "I will clean it up—later."

"Later? Why procrastinate?"

"It's my naptime."

"Fair enough," said Snake. "A good nap does wonders for the constitution. Shall I expect you afterward?"

"Not today. After my nap, it's dinnertime."

"Then when, may I inquire …"

"Later!" snapped Eve. She shooed the reptile away, fluffed up a nearby fern, and lay down for a nap.

"Well!" Snake exclaimed under his breath.

As Snake started home, he muttered to himself that something was quite amiss with the two "caretakers." He returned home, and as he descended into his den, he caught a glimpse of the key that had earlier fallen from the sky, denting his skull. Perhaps this key held the answer to his troubles.

"Using my superior powers of deduction, it is evident that this key must fit the padlock on the wrought-iron gate. After all, it is the only one in the garden."

Snake proceeded to the gate, where he tried the key in the lock and it opened.

"Fascinating," said Snake, as he stared at the Tree of Knowledge of Good and Evil. "This certainly is food for thought. I shall develop an appropriate course of action.

"Ah, a delicious solution," he chuckled to himself as he placed the key on the tree trunk before slithering out the gate. Snake shut the gate and clicked the lock closed on only one side of the gate. The gate looked locked but was not.

● ◗ ●

Sometime later while reclining in the warm afternoon sun, Eve said, "Adam, I've noticed Elephant is getting thinner. We need to build that bridge so she can get her peanuts."

"What? Yeah. Okay. First thing tomorrow," said Adam, who repositioned his face to catch more sun.

The next morning, tool chest in hand, Adam and Eve set out to build Elephant's bridge.

God smiled.

The angels, who up to this point had been wholly unimpressed with this species, reserved judgment.

Realizing he needed wood for the bridge, Adam cut a board from the tree lying across Snake's path, prompting Snake to regret the evil thoughts he had been harboring toward the man and woman.

After cutting the first board, Adam took a quick rest before starting on the second. When he sat down, he spotted some bright orange mushrooms lodged in the fallen tree's roots. He ate one. It was delicious. He popped one into Eve's mouth.

"Wow!" exclaimed Eve with the partially chewed mushroom in her mouth. "Let's find more!"

Adam packed his saw back into the toolbox. "The bridge can wait until later."

"Arrgghh!" cried Snake, twisting himself into a noose.

"Throw the bums out!" screamed the angels, demanding that God find new caretakers. The celestial beings went on strike and burst onto God's office cloud. Many held protest signs; some locked their wings to God's throne.

God was deaf to their pleas. "Listen, you think *you* got problems? You should only *look* at My To Do list. Believe Me, it could be worse. They could be pouring concrete all over the planet."

With that, God vanished in a pillar of fire. The angels muttered a bit before dropping their signs, unlocking their wings, and flying off.

The next morning Eve awoke with a strange feeling.

"Adam, I don't feel right."

"You shouldn't have eaten so many mushrooms."

"That's not it."

"Well, what is it?"

"I don't know. It's just that I feel sort of ... you know ... empty. You know what I mean?"

"You ate about a hundred mushrooms, and you feel empty," said Adam, shaking his head. "Listen, Bighorn Sheep just told me about some mountains that have this white stuff called snow. I'm going to check it out. Maybe snow tastes good. See you later."

So while Adam went off to the mountains, Eve tried to get rid of her emptiness by stuffing her stomach with as much food as she could cram into it. She then had a stomachache to accompany her emptiness. Snake, meanwhile, was moving ahead with his plan to speak with Eve, alone. Earlier, Snake had gathered leaves and twigs from the Tree of Knowledge of Good and Evil and cooked them into incense. Then he had instructed Bighorn Sheep to tell Adam about the mountains. Now with Adam gone, Snake lit the incense upwind from Eve. The delicious aroma filled her nostrils, and she dropped a cluster of grapes from her hands. Eve knew this scent, but from where? As if in a trance, she followed her nose as Snake led her through the garden. Eve closed her eyes to better home in on the scent. For protection she walked with her arms in front. Though Eve was immortal, slamming into trees still hurt.

Eve shuffled through the garden until she felt the presence of something in front of her. Eve stopped and slowly extended her hands until they gently touched two unfamiliar cylindrical surfaces that were cool, hard, and smooth. Eve opened her eyes and nearly forgot how to breathe when she saw her fingers clutching the bars of the wrought-iron gate. Wrapped around a branch of the Tree of Knowledge of Good and Evil was Snake.

Eve gripped the bars tightly because she was having trouble balancing on her wobbling knees.

Snake smiled. "Care to join me?"

Eve stared at Snake.

"No need for alarm. I don't bite. Are you not ... curious?"

"Adam will hit me if he finds me here," Eve said. "But even if I was ... curious, like you said, how could I get in? The gate's locked. I can't wriggle through like you."

"Push."

As if they had a mind of their own, her hands pushed the gate open, and there she was, inside.

"That was not terribly difficult, was it?"

"You tricked me!" yelled Eve, stilling her wobbly knees and straightening her back. "You want me to eat that fruit and die."

Snake smiled. "How astute."

Eve narrowed her eyes and proclaimed, "I will never even touch one."

"Catch." Snake tossed a fruit to Eve.

Again Eve's hands disobeyed her will, and Eve held the golden fruit between her palms. Its softness, texture, and fragrance threatened to overcome her. But instead of giving in to temptation, Eve threw it back to Snake.

"Three seconds," said Snake. "Your eternal vow regarding this exquisite food lasted three seconds."

"You're a dirty sneak," hissed Eve. "You can trick me into catching it, but you can't make me eat it." Snake rolled the fruit toward Eve. It came to rest next to her left foot.

"Eve, it is your uninformed impression that this is the Tree of Death, because once you eat from it, you will die. Yet, that is not its name. It is called the Tree of Knowledge of Good and Evil."

"So?" said Eve, wondering whether she should kick or squash the deadly thing.

"So if you ingest its produce, you will gain knowledge and become wise."

Eve folded her arms. "Adam was right. We don't need knowledge, and I don't want to be wise."

"You do not need the ability to discern good from evil? How can you live responsibly?"

"I live fine," said Eve. "Besides, if I eat it, I'll die."

"So?"

"So?" Eve repeated. "I told you. I don't want to die."

"Why not?"

Eve could not believe her ears. "Why not? Are you serious? When you die, you're ... you're dead," she explained, hoping to end this ridiculous discussion.

"Quite circular reasoning," said Snake. "Yes, my friend Eve, when you die, you are indeed dead. Yet, is death so terrible? Your soul returns to God. A not altogether distasteful experience, my sources inform me."

Eve was wavering. Luckily, she had one last argument, her trump card. It was her turn to grin.

"Nice try, Snake. But I can't die, because if I do, who will take care of the garden? *I* am the caretaker."

Eve flashed the smug smile of someone who threw down four aces and was about to collect the chips. She turned to walk out of the garden, the victor. Snake could eat his stupid fruit by himself. She was the caretaker.

"Fake!"

Eve looked back. "What? What did you say?"

"I said, 'fake,' although I suppose I could have substituted any number of synonyms: liar, phony, cheat, pretender, charlatan, impostor, quack. Yes, quack. I quite like the sound of that word. You, my friend Eve, are a quack. You are as much the garden's caretaker as I ... its highest jumper."

"Of course I'm the caretaker. God appointed me, and Adam too."

"Very well. Would you please be so kind as to inform me of a single caretaking task you have taken care of since your appointment?"

"Why I ... we ... I ..."

"Don't have anything to say," said Snake, finishing Eve's sentence. "Now, Eve, it must be clear even to you that if you have not performed the duty of the caretaker, you simply cannot call yourself the caretaker."

Eve stared blankly at Snake, who flicked his tongue and smelled victory. "I have been observing you, Eve. You have been somewhat depressed, am I not correct?"

Snake was right, she had been.

"The root cause of your melancholy stems from the realization that you do not actually live."

"I don't live?" Eve said. "That's ridiculous."

"One who is ignorant of her own mortality cannot fully live."

"What are you talking about?" Eve asked, but she was not sure she wanted an answer.

"If you have awareness that you will one day cease to be, each day is precious and you live. Without this knowledge, you cannot really live; you can only exist."

"Adam and I enjoy every day more than you ever could."

"Is enjoyment the sole function of living?"

Eve was now more confused. "This is crazy talk. You make no sense."

Snake's eyes moved to the fruit at Eve's foot. "There is one way to determine the truth of my words."

Eve looked down. Was Snake right? Could she only fill her emptiness by becoming mortal? Or was Snake simply jealous and determined to trick her because he wanted her to die? After all, Snake was a sneak.

Eve bent down and picked up the fruit. Its sweet smell suffused her from the top of her head to the soles of her feet. She wanted to eat it, she really did, but she was afraid. Snake did not utter another word. The angels held their breath. God stopped the wind.

Eve would have to take the final step herself.

It is not recorded how long they remained frozen in their spots. Perhaps a second, a minute, maybe even an entire day passed and not a muscle moved. Some events are beyond time.

"Eve!" Adam's voice broke the silence. "I just climbed this great mountain! Where are you? Let's eat! Did you know that snow is cold? It froze my lips! Listen to my funny whistle! Phhhttt! Where the heck are you?"

She bit.

At that exact moment, Adam walked by the open gate. "What the … the gate's open! Eve, what are you … *Did you lose your mind?!*"

Adam rushed in to grab Eve and force the fruit out of her.

He got within arm's reach and stopped. He was too late. Eve was no longer Eve, or rather, Eve was now truly Eve. Her eyes sparkled. That was new. Adam looked into her eyes and saw her soul. It had opened up, and Adam saw the whole universe inside. There was God smiling.

She offered. He ate.

* * *

"Remember," said God as Adam and Eve were putting the final touches on Elephant's bridge. "Don't overdo it. Work six days, rest on the seventh."

Eve looked at their endless work list and realized that they would never be able to fix everything before their deaths. She started to cry.

Adam put his hand on Eve's cheek and wiped away a tear. "Honey, don't worry. We'll just do the best we can, right?"

Eve nodded. "I guess you're right."

Adam stroked Eve's hair. "You know, since I ate that fruit, I've had this new feeling for you."

Eve took Adam's hand and kissed it. "And I for you."

"That's right," said God. "Have a good time. Make yourselves some kids. They'll finish up after you're gone."

God bid them farewell, and Adam and Eve went off to explore their new feelings. They were now mortal and wise and not about to waste their precious time, though Eve always took a moment to stop and smell a fragrant rose, and Adam never missed an opportunity to climb a particularly nice mountain.

Cain's
Co-Defendant

1 can't do it!" Eve screamed, tightening her fingers around Adam's wrist.

"You are doing fantastic," coaxed Snake. "Just one more push."

Eve took a huge breath and, with an Amazonian effort, pushed out the world's first human baby. Snake dabbed the sweat from her brow, Adam fainted, and a few moments later, Eve pushed out a second son.

Snake cut the umbilical cords, and Eve cuddled the twins in her arms. Her chest could barely contain her heart as she gazed first at one child and then at the other. For a long time, Eve had anticipated motherhood. Now that it was here, Eve knew it would be everything that she had hoped.

Adam, on the other hand, took to fatherhood like Lion to a bowl of lettuce. For the better part of a year, he watched Eve grow fatter and fatter. At first he thought she was sick and summoned Snake. Snake examined Eve and smiled, causing Adam to gnaw his fingernails to the cuticles. He knew from experience that whenever Snake smiled about something, it was time to start worrying.

Soon Eve was so fat that Adam commented, "You look like Hippo."

Eve gave Adam the first of many black eyes he was to receive over the coming months.

In the weeks following the twins' birth, Adam's life worsened. Not only did Eve completely ignore him, but the boys went through food faster than Hummingbird slurped nectar from a hillside of honeysuckles. Adam worked sunrise to sunset keeping his brood fed.

"If I knew this would have been the punishment for that Tree of Knowledge business," Adam groaned as he hauled a load of bananas, "I would never even have *touched* that fruit."

Though the boys, Cain and Abel, were twins, they were as different as Ant is from Whale. First, Cain. He had green eyes, black hair, and enormous hands. As a baby, Cain cracked coconuts by squeezing them between his hands.

One day after his fourth birthday, Cain saw Adam planting wheat and laughed.

"What are you laughing about?" demanded his father.

"You bury seeds like Dog bury bones."

"Don't be stupid," were the words that almost flew out of Adam's mouth, but they were stopped by a bright idea.

"These, my son," said Adam, putting his arm around Cain, "are magic seeds. If *you* water them every day, magic will happen."

Cain did so; one week later, seedlings sprouted. Cain proudly showed his father.

Adam said, "You did a good job; the magic started. Keep watering and now start weeding around the plants."

Cain happily agreed. When the wheat was ready, Cain, using his hands as sickles, harvested the crop. While watching his son hard at work, Adam reconsidered his initial feelings toward the children.

The next day a sad Cain came to Adam.

"What's up?" Adam asked.

"Miss plants."

"So plant more."

"No magic seeds."

Adam bent down and whispered into his son's ear, "All seeds are magic."

"All seeds magic?"

"You just have to water and care for them," said his father.

Cain smiled and went to work. The years passed and Cain grew to become a farming magician. Two people were needed to harvest a single cluster of his melon-sized grapes. His carrots were so large that Cain tied one end of a rope around the carrot top and the other around Elephant's neck, in order to pull the vegetable out of the ground.

Though Cain loved farming, he was often lonely. He was shy because language did not come easily to him. He wanted to say funny, witty things, but it was difficult to find the right words. More than anything, Cain wished that he could speak well and make friends like his brother, Abel.

Now to Abel. While Cain was green-eyed with black hair, Abel had a blond top and brown eyes. Cain was known for his hands. Abel's identifying feature was his mouth. It was cavernous. The cry that issued from his lips when he was born rousted Bear from hibernation and set off a series of small avalanches in the Himalaya Mountains.

Not to be outdone by Cain's coconut trick, Abel could crack the giant nut by crunching it between his teeth.

From the moment Abel emerged from the womb, he jabbered to anyone within listening range. He constantly pestered his parents with questions like: "Father, why do apples fall down from trees rather than rise up?" Or, "Mother, why are you getting more lines on your face?" Adam knew nothing about falling apples, and Eve was not thrilled about what was happening to her face, much less having it pointed out. Their usual reply was, "Don't ask so many questions."

The animals, on the other hand, were more patient and taught the boy the secrets of their lives. Abel learned why Goose flew south in the winter and how long Snake's skin lasted between sheddings. Spider taught him the art of web weaving, and Zebra explained the reason for his stripes. Abel loved the animals, and the animals loved him. At Cain and Abel's birthday parties, the animals congregated around Abel, who made them laugh with his animal impressions, such as imitating Lion's roar. Excluding the ungulates, everyone thought this a riot. In the corner of the party, Cain was usually eating birthday cake by himself.

While Cain worked hard providing the family with food, Abel was content to spend his days thinking new thoughts and conversing with his animal friends. At dinner he would share his insights with his family. For their part, the first family was unimpressed with their second son.

"Gravity? Who cares about gravity?" said Eve. "Juice the apples that fall on your head."

Adam concurred. "You think too much. Look at me. I hardly ever think. Am I suffering? If you ask me, thinking is overrated. Anyway, it's time for you to start pulling your weight around here."

"Yes," agreed Eve. "It's time you got a job."

The next day, while Abel was sitting under a shady tree thinking about possible employment, along came Sheep. Poor Sheep had never been shorn. At first glance, Abel thought Sheep was a tumbleweed, her wool was so long. The bush, however, spoke, and Abel spied two small eyes deep inside.

"Help," moaned a muffled voice. "I'm suffocating."

"Sheep?" asked Abel.

"Could you get me out of here?"

Abel obliged and within minutes a shorn Sheep stood beside a huge pile of wool.

"Burn it!" Sheep demanded, pointing a hoof at the pile.

Abel, however, was not ready to spark his flint. He knew wool was warm, and there were times when the weather was cold.

"If I can only figure out how to turn this wool into clothing."

Just then, he spied Spider spinning a web. Abel snapped his fingers. "That's it! I'll spin the wool into yarn and knit a shirt!"

Abel's first shirt was good for warm summer evenings, because, like Spider's web, it was mostly open space. Through trial and error, Abel learned to knit a decent sweater. Since Sheep's relations all needed shearing, Abel soon had enough wool to knit his family shirts, sweaters, socks, hats, pants, and underwear. Instead of finding one job, as his parents demanded, Abel found two—he was the world's first shepherd and its first tailor.

Abel loved his work because after the seasonal shearing, he had plenty of time to sit under trees, knit, eat coconuts, talk with his animal friends, and consider the relative merits of green and red apples.

Abel provided clothes, and Cain furnished food. Their parents approved, and life was blissful—until an angel mucked everything up.

●　◉　◉

One day God watched Cain and Abel exchange birthday presents. A bouquet of golden roses surrounded by orange irises and bright red lilies from Cain, a paisley wool tie in mauve and turquoise from Abel. God commented to Gabriella, the chief angel, "Such nice boys giving gifts."

Gabriella replied, "Hmm."

"What are you 'Hmm'ing about?" God asked.

"Open Your eyes," said Gabriella. "They give gifts to each other."

"Isn't that *exactly* what I just said?"

"But what have they ever given *You*? Nothing. Never a gift. Not even a single word of appreciation."

"Hmm. A little thank-you now and then would be nice."

"You want to know what I think?" said Gabriella. "I think they take You for granted."

"No, they're good boys," said God. "But maybe they could send up a tasty something."

Gabriella flew down to deliver the message.

- - -

"A sacrifice?" Abel could not believe his ears when Gabriella gave the brothers the message.

"The sooner the better," the angel replied before flying off.

Abel shook his head.

"I don't get it. God created everything, so why does God need something from us? God can make anything God wants. The whole thing is illogical. It doesn't make a bit of sense."

"I think maybe God lonely, want love," said Cain.

"God lonely?" Abel snickered. "That's what you think? Listen, brother, I think you better leave the thinking to me."

Cain looked to the ground and said, "Sometimes I lonely."

"If I talked to carrots all day, I'd be lonely, too."

No matter what Abel thought, Cain truly believed that God was lonely, and he figured that if he gave God a good sacrifice, God would be his friend. Abel figured that if he did not give God a good sacrifice, God might toss a lightning bolt at him. Both brothers got busy.

Abel chose his handsomest, most succulent lamb to sacrifice. While Abel sharpened his knife, Cain scratched his head. What should he sacrifice? Could God possibly want an extralarge carrot or an orange the size of a medium boulder? No. Even though Cain's fruits and vegetables were the best in the world, still they were things created by God. Cain figured that God would appreciate something made with Cain's own hands, like …

"Bread!" Cain exclaimed. "Nothing better than warm bread with butter on top."

Cain ground some wheat, kneaded the flour into dough, formed a twelve-braided loaf, and put it into his oven. While the bread baked, Cain helped Abel slaughter and roast the lamb.

"Mmm, that's good," said God and accepted the sacrifice. Abel smiled at Cain.

Cain prayed, "God, be happy with bread."

"Something's burning," said Abel, "and it's not lamb."

Cain looked and saw dark smoke billowing from the oven. Cain had been so busy helping Abel that he forgot to check the bread. A hard, black mess stood in place of his beautiful loaf.

"Don't worry," Abel said. "It's the thought that counts. Put the leftover wheat on the altar. God will accept it."

Cain took Abel's advice, but the wheat just sat there. His face dropped and tears filled his eyes.

Abel put his arm around his brother, but Cain threw it off, knocking Abel over.

"No wonder you don't have any friends," Abel said.

Cain cursed the injustice. Everyone liked Abel, but he was no better than Cain. Now even God took Abel's side. His face tightened into a clenched fist.

"Why not You like me?" thundered Cain to heaven.

"Not like you?" God replied. "I love you like a son. Listen, why don't you bake another loaf? Or maybe make some granola.

But, Cain, you better watch that temper. Now *that's* trouble. Better keep an eye on it."

"I hate You!" Cain screamed at the top of his voice and added under his breath, "and Abel, too."

The next day Cain found his brother in the field and offered him a big slice of strawberry.

Cain said, "For yesterday."

"Forget it. You were upset. I should have left you alone."

"Okay," said Cain. "Listen, I have question. What you think happen after Mother and Father die?"

"Can't say I've given it a moment's thought," replied Abel, devouring the strawberry.

Cain said, "I thinking."

"That's a surprise," said Abel, raising an eyebrow and spitting out a seed.

"When they die we only ones in world. I thinking me and you divide world now. I farmer and need land."

Abel sucked on his teeth and said, "That was some strawberry."

Cain continued, "You shepherd and need sheep."

"Right you are," said Abel.

"So I get land. You get things move on land," suggested Cain.

Abel thought about the idea, and it seemed to make some sense, but something was not quite—kosher. Since when was Cain coming up with plans? But Abel could not figure out what bothered him, so he said, "Why not?"

They shook hands to seal the deal. Abel returned to contemplate why an apple that is twice as heavy as a second apple falls at the same rate and not twice as fast as the lighter apple.

Suddenly, Cain kicked Abel's foot.

"Off my land!" yelled Cain.

"What are you kicking me for, turnip brain!"

"Land mine! Leave!"

Abel threw his apple at Cain. But when he saw the look in Cain's eyes, Abel jumped up and ran. Cain chased his brother through the field and grabbed him when Abel tripped over a rock. Cain put his hands around Abel's throat and throttled him. Abel twisted, opened his mouth, and chomped down on Cain's left arm. Cain screamed, but Abel clamped down even harder. With his free hand, Cain let Abel go and found the rock that tripped Abel. He grabbed it and smashed Abel on the head. Abel released Cain's arm and lay still.

God watched in silence.

Cain held his wounded arm and called to his brother, "Forget deal. Bad idea."

Abel did not answer.

"I say forget it. Sit where you want. You bite hard."

Cain saw blood leaking from Abel's head. He shook him, nothing. He bent over Abel's face, nothing. The breath of life was gone. Abel was dead. What should he do? His parents would be angry. Cain took a shovel and dug a large hole. He gently put Abel's body into the hole and covered it with dirt.

After compacting the earth, Cain dropped the shovel, wiped away the sweat, and wept on his brother's grave.

●　●　●

Daniel, the angel of justice, addressed God: "Cain has clearly violated the Sixth Commandment, 'Thou Shall Not Murder.' With Your permission, I request a trial."

God wiped a tear and nodded.

One day later, Cain was ushered into heaven's courtroom. The jury consisted of angels from the far reaches of the universe.

The prosecutor, Daniel, sat at one table, Cain at another. Seated on a throne of clouds was God, holding a gavel fashioned from a lightning bolt.

The bailiff asked Cain to stand. "Cain, son of Adam and Eve, you are accused of murdering your brother, Abel. How do you plead?"

"Not guilty."

Daniel jumped from his seat. "Not guilty? Then how do you explain your fingerprints and Abel's blood on that?" Daniel pointed to the rock.

"Your brother," said God. "Do you know where he is?"

"I my brother keeper? You God. You know where."

"Yes, I know," said God. "The voice of your brother's blood cries out to Me from the ground. Cain, what have you done?"

Cain looked down at the hands in his lap. "You right. I kill him."

Daniel pounced. "Ah ha! You admit it! Murderer!" Turning to the jury he announced, "I seek the death penalty."

Cain raised his head.

"I kill him, but I not murderer."

Daniel chortled. "You, who crushed your innocent brother's skull, are not the murderer? Then please kindly inform the court as to who is."

Cain stood up, slowly raised his arm, and pointed at God.

"God?" spluttered Daniel. "Is this your idea of a sick joke?"

Cain walked to the evidence table, picked up the rock, and said, "How I know rock kill Abel when hit on head? I not try kill him, want him let go." Cain stared at the rock. "Okay, I want hurt him, but not kill."

Cain turned to God. "Why You not stop me? You villain. You not protect Abel."

"It's not My job to interfere," God said.

The jury nodded in agreement. God had given humans

free will. They had the ability to choose between right and wrong, good and evil. Of course God wanted them to choose good, but if they chose evil, even if there were tragic consequences, it was not God's fault.

Cain shook his head. "Not true. You reason I hate Abel, because You love him, not me. You say You not interfere. Not true. You do. You make me hate."

Cain stared at the rock in his hand.

"I not happy I kill Abel."

His lower lip trembled and his eyes watered.

"Daniel right. I guilty." Cain lifted his eyes from the rock to God and added, "You guilty too."

Cain sat down. The courtroom buzzed. God rapped the gavel.

"Order! Order in this court!"

Daniel approached the throne, turned toward Cain, and said, "God, with Your permission, I will have the bailiff remove this insubordinate, offensive, obstinate, and despicable human from Your presence."

God ignored Daniel and said, "It is true that I created humans in My image, and it is also true that humans are not perfect ..."

"You not perfect?" Cain interrupted.

"Uh—well—think of Me more like a diamond that's still a little rough around the edges. But it was you, Cain, who hit Abel with the rock, not Me. I warned you, but you didn't listen."

Cain stared at God.

God continued, "I will not, however, recommend the death penalty."

God dismissed the jury to deliberate. Three minutes later, they returned and the foreangel announced, "We have reached our verdict. Through your own admission, we find you, Cain, son of Adam and Eve, guilty of murder. The punishment: the land, despoiled by the blood of Abel, will no longer yield produce for you. Your life as a farmer is finished. You wanted all the land, now you will have none. You will spend the rest of your days wandering the earth without a home."

God nodded.

Cain said, "What about God?"

"What about God?" the foreangel replied.

"God not guilty?"

"You were on trial, not God. Be gone."

Cain caught God's eye. God turned away.

●　◍　◉

The wandering began in the desert to the east of Eden. Cain arrived at an oasis where Camel was drinking water. Camel fled when he saw Cain. A little later, Raven pooped on Cain's head. That night Cain made a fire and did not close his eyes for fear that Scorpion or some other animal might try to kill him.

Morning came. The lack of sleep and fear of attack caused Cain to bellow at the rising sun, "This punishment too big to bear!"

God heard Cain and placed a mark on Cain's head to protect him from the animals. Whoever would harm Cain would have to answer to God.

Cain said to God, "Now You care, but You still guilty. My children will not forget. Some will not love You, because You not there when needed. Others will say You not even exist."

God saw the truth in Cain's prophecy, and a single tear fell down God's cheek.

Noah's Cracked
Rainbow

S aturn-sized rings appeared under God's eyes. Night after
night the Creator suffered from insomnia worrying about
Earth. While swigging a second cup of morning coffee, God
heard a loud commotion, looked down, and saw a walled city
surrounded by soldiers.

Milchama, the attacking general, called up to the city,
"Bow down to our god, or I'll level this stinking cesspool."

A fusillade of arrows rained down from the city, and
Milchama's soldiers stormed the walls.

"I can't stand it!" God cried.

"Hmm?" responded the chief angel, Gabriella, her nose in
a newspaper.

"They're killing each other over *Me!*"

Gabriella dipped a biscuit into her latte and replied, "Oh?"

"Oh?" repeated God. "Every single day they rob, rape, torture, and kill each other, and you give Me 'Oh?'"

Gabriella drained her latte, folded her paper, flicked the
crumbs from her fingers, and said, "I seem to remember making
my views known on this matter when You first told me about
creating a mortal being in Your image. I said, 'Mistake. Too much
power for a bit of blood and bones.'

"I'm only surprised that it took You this long to realize that
I was right. See You later. I'm off."

"Wait," said God, "I need some advice. What I should do?"

"If I were You, which happily I am not, I'd drown them all and write the whole thing off as a loss. You know, You look like Death. You need a vacation." Gabriella unfurled her wings and flew off.

God sighed. "She's right. Humans were a mistake. They turned the gifts of power and creativity into a curse. They're mean. And now the other animals are imitating their ways. Everything has to go. That vacation will have to wait."

While it was true that Earth was filled with evil, there was one innocent man named Noah. He never robbed anyone, he went out of his way to avoid fighting, and he loved God. In addition, Noah was a terrific baker. Every morning he looked up into the heavens, and said, "Morning, God! How about a fresh cinnamon bun?"

It so happened that at the very moment God decided to drown all life, a whiff of warm cinnamon wafted by. God froze. The weather stopped.

"Noah," God whispered. "What about Noah?"

Like a baby too young to understand his parents' words but who knows when something is amiss, Noah said, "Everything okay up there?"

God waved a hand and started a small breeze. Satisfied all was right, Noah went on his way.

The next time God saw Gabriella, God said, "What about Noah? He's innocent. I can't drown him."

"Look," she said, adjusting her halo, "out of the hordes of human beings, there is bound to be a decent guy. But You know as well as I that, as a species, they're loathsome. Sooner You obliterate the whole batch, the better."

"Collective punishment isn't right," God said, pacing up and down a cloud. "I got it! I'll save Noah; he can repopulate the world with good people. It's all in the genes."

Gabriella sighed. "You never give up."

"That's why I'm God," said God.

"How are You planning to save Your precious little man? Give him a boat?"

"Boat, yes. Give, no. Let *him* build an ark; he can save some of the animals too."

Gabriella shrugged her wings and went to research precipitation patterns and ground absorption rates. God tested a variety of woods for seaworthiness before calling on Noah.

• ◖ •

Noah was napping when he heard a soft, "Noah." He looked to the right. Nothing. He looked to the left. Nothing. He returned to his nap.

"Hey, Noah. Up here."

Noah looked up and—lo and behold—standing on a cloud emanating a brilliant golden light was God, Ruler of the Universe, holding a set of blueprints.

"Who are you?" asked Noah.

"Who am I? Who do you think? I'm God."

Noah fell on his face and said, "Your unworthy servant is at Your command."

"Got any bagels?"

Noah quickly fetched one.

"Thanks," said God. "Listen, I've got good news and bad news."

In a shaky voice Noah asked, "W-w-what's the bad news?"

"I'm going to destroy your entire species. You're a spiteful bunch who treat each other and the rest of Creation like yesterday's garbage. I'm going to drown the lot of you."

God surveyed the bagel. "Have any cream cheese?"

"All of us?" spluttered Noah.

"The good news is that I'm saving you." God paused and added, "How about a slice of tomato too?"

Noah fetched the cream cheese and tomato.

God continued, "Now listen closely. Here are the blueprints for you to build an ark. When you finish, take your family and the animals on it. Then the drowning will commence. Got it?"

"Sure, but what's an ark?"

"It's in the blueprints. They explain everything. I'll see you later."

God whistled and a fiery chariot whisked God away.

* * *

It was slow work constructing the ark, yet plank by plank, peg by peg, a great boat began to appear. Noah's wife made a list of all the animal species and their numbers. After calculating for six weeks, she discovered that to save all Earth's animals, the ark would have to be as big as modern-day Texas. Though the ark was large, the size of a couple of football fields lying end to end, this discovery worried Noah. He called God for a point of clarification.

Gabriella came down.

"God, is that You?" Noah asked.

"God's busy settling a tiff between the Seven Sisters," Gabriella replied. "They're sick of each other and want to start their own galaxies."

The angel let out a whistle. "That is some ark."

"I think there's a problem," Noah said. "It's going to be too small to carry all the animals on Earth."

Gabriella made a quick calculation on her fingers and realized he was right. She scratched her halo and computed a little more calculus, thermodynamics, and specific relativity before letting out a big "Ah-ha!"

"You're not supposed to bring *all* the animals. God planned for you to bring only a pair of each species, a male and female. If you do that, you'll have enough space with a little room to spare. If I were you, which happily I am not, I'd bring a few sacrificial animals to thank God for saving your life. Personally, I recommended that he destroy everybody."

Gabriella shot Noah a malevolent grin and flew off.

●　●●　●

Day after day, week after week, month after month, Noah worked on the ark. Every day people flowed by asking why he was building a gigantic boat in the middle of the desert.

"I think it's going to be a pretty rainy season," was his standard reply.

The people shrugged their shoulders, and Noah resumed hammering. How come Noah didn't tell the truth? Perhaps when faced with the upcoming catastrophe, the people might have changed their evil ways.

Noah kept his mouth shut because he didn't think anyone would believe him. Rather, he thought they would mock him, maybe even burn the ark.

"Even if they believe me," Noah told himself, "can a tiger change his stripes? People can't change who they are, so what's the point? In the end, they're going to drown anyway."

A relatively dry winter came and went, and the community decided to find out what was really up with Noah's boat.

They stormed the ark and found Gabriella instructing

Noah on framing the windows. Noah gulped as the horde eddied around the ark.

"See you later," said Gabriella. "All these humans make me break out."

Noah cried, "What should I do?"

"Tell them the truth," she said, and she flew off.

God nodded and thought, "Maybe if they know the consequences of their hate, they'll be nice to each other, and I won't need to drown them."

The crowd swamped Noah.

Noah cleared his throat and announced, "The truth is that God is going to drown all the bad people in the world. I'm building this ark to save the innocent."

Upon hearing their death sentences, not a single man or woman repented or screamed or fainted or did anything but give an approving grunt. To a person, they all believed that the world was going pretty badly. A good overhaul was in order. And every single person believed that he or she would be among those sailing on the ark. So rather than searching their souls, changing their ways, and pleading for God's mercy, the people were wondering about their chances for window seats.

● ▬ ●

After Noah sealed the inside with pitch, the ark was finally finished. Gabriella inspected it, pronounced it seaworthy, and gave Noah a list of animal food. Noah grimaced. Just when he thought he was finished, another huge job for the six-hundred-year-old man. But there was nothing to do but start collecting ants for the aardvarks. Three months later Noah finished gathering bunch grass for the zebras, and he was ready to load his passengers. Pairs of animals lined up. Noah checked them off as Gabriella called them up the gangplank.

"Bears," said Gabriella.

"Check," said Noah.

"Beavers."

"Check."

"Bedbugs."

"Bedbugs?"

"Bedbugs."

Noah sighed and waved them on as he scratched an imaginary bite.

"Bees."

"Check."

Noah's neighbors stood by with their bundled possessions. Gabriella told them to wait until the animals had boarded. They became uncomfortable when they saw that bad people were also waiting in line. If their neighbors, who they knew were bad, thought they were good, the people all reasoned, then could they, who thought they were good, actually be bad?

Every person examined his or her own life. One man saw that he spent too little time with his children, and they grew up troubled and distant. A woman realized how often she had closed her eyes to beggars. A family remembered that they threw their garbage in the stream behind their home.

Every person looked deep within, and every person found a human being who could have been better, much better. The people understood why God was angry, and they all vowed to change their ways. They prayed to God for forgiveness and began acting kindly to each other.

God watched and thought about giving the doomed a second chance.

Meanwhile, the animals kept coming.

"Turtles."

"Check."

"Unicorns."

"Check."

"Voles."

"Check."

The animals were almost loaded when it became clear to the assemblage that room on the ark was rapidly running out. The entire crowd, who only moments before had vowed to change their lives for the better, stormed the ark pushing, elbowing, and stampeding toward the gangplank.

Gabriella sailed above the rioters holding a gigantic mirror to let the would-be passengers see themselves as they really were. They looked up at their ugly reflections and understood that all was lost; the sky began to drizzle.

The yaks, yellow jackets, and zebras quickly filed in, and Noah shut the ark door. The heavens opened wide and the rains poured out of the clouds.

The floodwaters quickly rose and soon all life, save those on the ark, perished. God cried and Gabriella even managed a sniffle, and Noah—well, Noah had too much on his hands to worry about anyone else. Tempers flared between the animals, and Noah found himself breaking up fights every day. Then there was the tragedy of the unicorns.

The raccoons, which were sleek and proud animals, were bored with their berry diet. Noah had forgotten to pack meat for these omnivores. After a week on the ark, they started craving breast of unicorn.

Late one night the raccoons picked the lock on their pen. They quickly and silently snuck over to the unicorn pen. Knowing that unicorns loved bangles on their horns, the raccoons offered them some. Vanity overtook fear, and the stag came close enough for one raccoon to jump onto his back and kill him. The raccoons dragged the carcass to their pen. Next morning when Noah came around with breakfast, the raccoons were sleeping off their feast. Noah cursed them and God changed the raccoons into lumbering beasts destined to spend eternity scavenging through garbage cans.

After forty days Noah said, "This ark smells like a cesspool. The animals are getting crankier by the hour. And I, I need some sun. If this doesn't end soon, I'll go mad and throw myself overboard."

God had mercy on Noah and stopped the rain. The waters receded and the ark came to rest on Mount Ararat.

A week later, Noah thought about sending the animals out. First, however, he needed to know if the land was dry. He called in Raven.

Raven glided into Noah's cabin and made himself comfortable on a couch.

"Hey, man," said Raven. "What's the plan? No offense, but this is the smelliest ark I've ever been on."

"I need you to scout the land and tell me if it's safe for the animals to leave."

Raven cracked his neck in thought.

"Now don't take this wrong, man. But while I sincerely thank you for the cruise, I, Raven, am not—I repeat—am not your bird."

Raven hopped to the door and would have left had Noah not grabbed his wing.

"What do you mean, you're not my bird," demanded Noah.

"Hey, let go, man ..."

"That's Noah," said Noah.

"No disrespect, but this is a dangerous mission. Say something happens and I—you know—croak. What then? Me and the missus are endangered. There's only two of us. If I die, that's it. No more ravens. Look, man ..."

"It's Noah!"

"Whatever. Hey, I'm just trying to help. Why not send one of those nice sacrificial doves. You got seven pairs of them. No disrespect to doves, but—hey—lose one, no big deal."

Noah ignored Raven's argument, opened the window, and tossed out the bird. Raven flew all over Earth before returning to report that water was still everywhere. A week later, Noah, taking Raven's advice, sent out Dove. Like Raven, Dove found only water. One week later, Dove went out again and found muddy land littered with millions of uprooted trees and countless corpses. The air stank of death. Everywhere Dove flew, the ruin was total.

Disheartened, Dove was on her way back to the ark when she caught a whiff of fresh air. Dove tracked the scent to its source and found a single gnarled olive tree sprouting new growth. Earth was reborn. Dove plucked a twig and returned to Noah.

The next day the animals left the ark. While happy to be alive, they were worried.

"Will God do it again?" was the unspoken question on every lip and beak.

When Noah emerged from the ark, he made sacrifices to God.

God said to Gabriella, "I hate to admit it, but you might be right. From the moment humans are old enough to know good from bad, they do bad. But," God added, savoring Noah's sacrifice, "they have their moments. Good or bad, they're Mine. I promise never again to destroy Earth because of them.

"Write Me a memo and stick it over My desk. Then when they get Me mad, I won't forget My promise."

Gabriella shook her head. "Easier to find light in a black hole than anything in Your office. You'll never see the memo."

"Hmm," God concurred.

Gabriella snapped her wings and said, "Put Your bow in the sky. If You ever decide to drown them, You'll see Your bow and remember."

"Perfect!" God exclaimed.

God explained the bow idea to the animals. They breathed a collective sigh of relief, with the exception of Owl, who thought, "What if God decides to burn us with fire instead of drowning us in a flood? Since God can only see the bow when water is in the sky, how will God be reminded of the promise?"

Owl kept these thoughts to herself while the animals celebrated their new lives. She resolved to say something to Noah afterward. Unfortunately, she slept through the next day and never said anything.

● ━ ●

While thankful for his own rescue, Noah could not get the others out of his mind. Were they really so bad and he so good?

Noah kept thinking, "I should have helped them change their ways, or at least I should have begged God to save them." To ease his mind, Noah planted a vineyard, for wine always made him feel better.

Focused on his own misery, Noah ignored his family. Even before the Flood, his son Ham was trouble. Had it not been for his father's merit, Ham would have perished with the others. While on the ark, Noah had vowed to help Ham change his ways. But after the Flood, he did not.

When the grapes matured, Noah bottled their juice. When the wine was ready, he drank. After the first bottle, Noah felt rejuvenated and he remembered Ham. He called his son over. There was so much to tell him. They drank a bottle and told jokes. They drank another bottle and laughed out loud. They drank a third bottle, and the drunken Noah passed out on his bed. Ham ripped off his father's clothing and abused him. Noah's other sons, Shem and Japheth, discovered what had happened and covered their father with a blanket. When Noah awoke, he roared at Ham for the evil that he had done. Noah cursed both his son and his son's offspring.

The Flood failed to purge evil from the human species.

● ◑ ●

While Noah lived quietly for 350 more years, the real drama of humanity was played out between his sons. Like Noah, Shem and Japheth were good, righteous people. Ham, however, was evil. The sons fought all the time—good versus evil. Following their deaths, the battle continued to rage between their children throughout the generations. In fact, the struggle still rages today with the added complication that over the years the descendants intermarried. Today, all human beings have the blood of each one of Noah's children flowing through their veins.

Reasonable
Faith

Before sunrise, Terach tucked his knife into his leather belt. The elderly man stumbled as he lifted a large bundle of wood. A servant came to help, but Terach himself placed the wood on the donkey. Terach signaled to his eldest son Haran. The two of them walked east into the blood-red dawn, toward the canine-toothed mountains in the distance. Behind them followed two servants with a donkey.

When the men passed the village well, fourteen-year-old Sarai set her jug down and watched them until the rising sun swallowed them up.

Next to Sarai stood Haran's mother, Emtelai. She, too, watched.

"Emtelai, are they going to sacrifice?"

Emtelai wiped a tear from her eye, picked up her jug, and started off in the direction of her tent.

Sarai sensed that something was wrong. Terach had brought wood, fire, and his knife—everything he needed to make a sacrifice, everything, that is, except the sacrificial animal. Sarai's mother called her. She picked up her jug and returned to her family tent.

One week later, Terach, the two servants, and the donkey returned. As Terach passed Sarai, she saw spots of blood on his knife's bone handle. A wave of nausea swept through Sarai, and she emptied the contents of her stomach.

Haran's brother, a young man named Abram, gently put his hand on the small of Sarai's back.

"Are you okay?"

Sarai straightened up, searched Abram's face, and muttered, "Why?"

Abram did not reply. Instead, he escorted the shaky Sarai to her tent. When they arrived, Sarai's mother was there.

"Tea will do you well, my daughter." She turned to Abram and asked, "Will you join us?"

Sarai's mother put the kettle on the fire. The three sat in silence until the water boiled. Sarai's mother removed the kettle from the fire and poured a handful of mint leaves into the water.

"Why did Terach do it?"

Sarai's mother put the kettle on a low table between the three.

"Why wasn't I told?"

"Daughter, your ears were not yet ready to hear."

"My ears can hear anything."

Sarai's mother pointed to the kettle. "You see the pot, my daughter, but fail to recognize the mint inside. Yes, Terach sacrificed Haran. But it was not murder. We depend on the gifts of the gods to bring rain, to make our plants grow, to fill our wombs with new life. Without these great gifts our village would disappear. Do you believe that we deserve these gifts for free? Are we not responsible to give the gods what they desire?"

"So let him sacrifice a ram," Sarai answered.

Sarai's mother poured the steaming tea. "Terach is our chief. He is responsible for the village. He must bring a gift to the great god Moloch. He must bring the biggest gift he can, that which is most precious to him, his son. Only then will Moloch be satisfied and bless us with rain and fertility. You see, by giving up that which is dearest to him, Terach has ensured prosperity for all."

Sarai's mother offered a cup to her daughter.

"Drink, Sarai. It will settle your stomach."

Sarai ignored the cup. "And Haran? What about his prosperity?"

"Haran agreed to the sacrifice. Listen, Sarai, it is because of Moloch that I have children. Haran made a great sacrifice for our village, so that one day you too will be blessed with children. It is the way of the world."

Sarai stood up and left the tent. Abram followed her.

Sarai said, "Killing your son is wrong. Do you not agree?"

Abram cleared his throat and announced, "I do not believe in Moloch. There is only one God, Adonai."

"Yes," replied Sarai. "You have told me of your Adonai before. But the sacrifice. What about that?"

"Adonai does not require the blood of sons."

"Then Adonai will be my God."

One year later Abram and Sarai married. On their wedding day Abram sacrificed his best lamb to ensure that God would open Sarai's womb. He repeated the sacrifice a year later and then again every following year. Time passed and Sarai remained barren.

Rather than place her trust solely in Adonai, Sarai took matters into her own hands. She visited the medicine woman, who gave her special herbs to strengthen her womb. The midwife instructed Sarai to visualize a baby in her belly and time her sexual relations to her ovulation cycle. And every dawn, Sarai bathed her face in the rays of the rising sun and prayed to Adonai for a child. But every month, Sarai's cycle ended in blood.

The years went by and Sarai stopped using the herbs.

Sometime later she stopped charting her fertile times. Finally, Sarai stopped praying.

At dusk one evening when Sarai's niece Shira was showing off her newborn son at the village well, Sarai walked to the edge of the village and stared out to the west. She felt a hand on her shoulder. She turned to face Abram.

"You are troubled, Sarai."

Sarai buried her head against Abram's chest.

"I will never have children."

Abram stroked her hair.

"You will have children. Have faith in Adonai."

"My faith has disappeared like the setting sun."

"Perhaps your faith will return with the sunrise."

Sarai smiled, thinking that Abram's belief in Adonai was so innocent, so pure, so naïve; his understanding no different than a child's.

"Perhaps," she replied.

⬤ ⬤ ⬤

"Sarai," Abram said one morning upon waking, "I had a vision."

Sarai stared into her cup of tea. This was not her husband's first vision.

"God has instructed me to leave our village, go forth from our homeland, and travel to a new land, a land where God promises to make me a great nation."

"You and your visions," Sarai said, addressing her cup.

Abram took Sarai's cup, placed it on the table, and lifted Sarai's face to his. "This was different. I was truly touched by God."

Sarai looked into Abram's face. It glowed as if a fire burned beneath the parchment of skin. This was new. Sarai walked outside and took in the panorama of the only land she had ever known, hills of pasture bordered by the distant peaks. Could there be something in the air, in the water, in the dirt of this land that kept her childless?

She looked at her spotted, bony hands. Stupid, she told herself, you are an old woman. But hadn't she heard stories of older women suckling babies? Sarai looked at the goatskin tents of her village. There went Malka. Every day since they were children, the two had met when the sun was high to exchange gossip. They knew each other better than their husbands did. And now, Sarai asked herself, I should leave her? Might as well leave a part of my body, a piece of my soul. And for what? For one tiny spark of impossible hope?

Sarai envisioned the dangers and discomforts of a long journey to an unknown place where even a cup of decent tea was not guaranteed. She shook her head and sighed. At that moment, her niece Shira walked by, proudly watching her young son take his first steps. The glow on her face rivaled that of Abram's. Sarai's tiny spark caught fire. Where there is no risk, there is no life.

Sarai returned to Abram and said, "When do we leave?"

● ⬭ ◎

Two weeks later, Abram, Sarai, their servants, their animals, and all their possessions were crossing a river on the trek to the new land. Sarai twisted her ankle on a rock and fell face first into the water. A servant caught her and helped her the rest of the way across.

Sarai sat on the riverbank, examined her bruised ankle, and said, "I was wrong. Beginning anew is for newlyweds, not for a couple old enough to be waited upon by grandchildren."

Yet, Sarai persevered and they arrived in the land of Canaan, where fields upon fields of wheat and barley grew alongside pomegranate, fig, date, and olive orchards. They crossed into a valley filled with massive oaks and pregnant grapevines, unloaded their belongings, and pitched their tents.

Once the couple were settled in their new home, Abram told Sarai of a vision.

"Sarai, Adonai has blessed us with new names, Abraham and Sarah."

Sarai listened to her husband's vision, changed her name to Sarah, but with each passing month, her impatience with both Abraham and Adonai grew.

One day Abraham told her that God promised him descendants as numerous as the sands on the shore and the stars in the sky. Sarah replied, "Abraham, you're a man of great faith, but no reason. Look at me. I'm an old woman. It is impossible for me to bear children. My monthly cycles have ceased. Your visions and your Adonai are false."

Abraham was silent. Sarah turned from her husband and shifted her attention back to the cooking fire.

More years passed. One autumn morning, Abraham ran into Sarah's tent and asked her to quickly make a meal for three visitors. Sarah did so and then returned to her tent. The visitors were conversing outside. Sarah listened as one of the men told Abraham that Sarah would give birth to a son within a year. Sarah burst out laughing. After all, she was nearly ninety years old. Her arms were still clutching her belly when the tent flap opened, and a bright light streamed into the tent. The powerful ray was not sunlight; rather, it emanated from the visitor's face. Sarah was afraid.

"Why did you laugh?" he asked. "Is anything too difficult for God?"

"I did not laugh," Sarah lied.

"You did. You are a woman of little faith."

The visitor removed a small leather bag from his belt and handed it to Sarah.

"This will strengthen your faith."

The visitor left. Sarah opened the bag and poured the contents into her hand. The dried herbs smelled faintly of pomegranate. She heated a pot of water, steeped the herbs, and drank the tea. A little more than nine months later, Sarah gave birth to a son she named Isaac, "laughing boy."

Sarah said, "God has brought me laughter. Who would have believed that Sarah would suckle a child. Yet, here he is."

Eight days after the birth, Abraham took the bone-handled knife his father, Terach, had given him and circumcised Isaac's foreskin. Initially, Sarah recoiled, but she comforted herself with the thought that sacrificing a foreskin to God was clearly better than sacrificing the entire boy.

II

Before sunrise, Isaac's father tucked his knife into his leather belt. The elderly man stumbled as he lifted a large bundle of wood. A servant came to help, but his father himself placed the wood on the donkey. His father signaled Isaac, and the two of them walked east into the blood-red dawn, toward the canine-toothed mountains in the distance. Behind them followed two servants with a donkey.

Three days later they arrived at the foot of a mountain. His father told the servants to wait with the donkey for their return. He slung the fire pouch around his neck and touched the knife on his belt. Isaac carried the wood on his back, and the two men, one elderly and one young, climbed the mountain.

Usually when Isaac accompanied his father, his father would teach him about Adonai. On this journey, however, his father had been uncommonly quiet. Now that they were climbing the mountain, his father seemed completely lost in his thoughts.

"Father?"

"Yes, my son."

"I know that you have explained it to me before, but I still do not understand how a sacrifice professes our faith in God."

"To sacrifice," his father said, "to give up that which is important to you, is to put God above all else in your life. That, my son, is faith."

They continued climbing. As they approached the summit, Isaac felt a queasiness in his stomach. Something was wrong.

"Father?"

"Yes, my son."

"Forgive me for speaking again, but I see only the fire and the wood. Where is the ram for the sacrifice?"

His father stumbled and Isaac caught him. The two of them faced each other.

"God will see to the ram, my son."

The two of them continued together.

Father and son arrived on a mountaintop that overlooked the land of Canaan. Isaac's father removed the wood from Isaac's back. Together they built an altar out of rocks. Together they laid the wood on the altar. Isaac's father wiped the sweat from his brow and picked up the rope.

"Isaac?"

"Yes, Father."

"What is your most precious possession?"

Isaac tilted his head and looked into his father's wet eyes.

"Father, I possess nothing but my own life."

The corners of his father's mouth rose slightly above his pursed lips. "My son, your life is my most precious possession, too."

Isaac noticed his father's fingers tighten around the rope,

and he understood why there was no sacrificial animal. He was the ram, his life proof of his father's faith, as well as a test of his own. Isaac stared at the bone-handled knife tucked into his father's belt and swallowed.

"Tie me up, Father. I am ready to prove my faith."

Isaac climbed on top of the wood, and his father bound his arms to his sides. Isaac looked up into the sky, hoping that his sacrifice would purify his soul and bring him close to God. His father raised his hand, but when Isaac saw a glint of sun reflect off the knife's blade his faith stumbled. He strained against the knots with his bound hands.

"Father!" he screamed, but his father's face with its locked jaw and focused eyes showed no sign of hearing him. Isaac shut his eyes and braced himself.

III

The morning Abraham and Isaac left for the mountain, Sarah arose to find neither husband nor son about. Her servant reported that the two had gone to sacrifice.

"If it makes them feel better to sacrifice a ram to Adonai," Sarah said, "then so be it. But does God really desire the aroma of burning meat? Of course not. Better to clothe the naked, feed the hungry, and care for the sick. These are the sacrifices God appreciates."

Sarah then took a stack of flour cakes and curds to an ill neighbor.

Three days later, Sarah went to the flock to select a lamb for the meal she would make when Abraham and Isaac returned. There in the middle of the flock was the ram that Abraham had earlier designated for sacrifice.

Sarah quickly turned to the shepherd. "Did your master take a sacrificial animal from the flock?"

"No, ma'am. The master did not."

The nausea that she experienced so many years before returned as a tidal wave crashing over Sarah.

"Isaac," she whispered. And then again, softer, "Isaac."

Sarah pointed her walking stick toward the sky.

"A cruel joke!" she yelled. "That is what You have made of my life. You cut Your promise from my heart. Why was I brought into this world? Better I had never been born, than this."

Sarah lost her balance and fell hard, her desire to live flowing through the tears into the dirt under her face. Like a mortally wounded animal protecting her young, Sarah gathered her last energy for a single, focused lashing out. She stood up, faced the mountains, and wailed in a voice that sent sound waves reverberating throughout the heavens, "Abraham!" And then again, louder, "Abraham!"

Sarah's words carried her soul into the ether, as her lifeless body crumpled to the ground.

IV

Isaac held his breath as his tensed body anticipated the knife. His heart pounded under his ribs. A moment passed. From nearby a dove cooed. Isaac opened his eyes. The knife was no longer poised above his heart. He exhaled. His father was staring off in the distance, eyes unfocused. A white light blazed from his face. A shudder went through his father's body, and his eyes moved to Isaac.

Isaac felt the knife cut through the ropes that bound him.

His father said, "I have just heard the voice of the true God call my name. Adonai does not require your sacrifice."

His father smiled broadly and extended a hand to help Isaac down. "My faith was strong. I passed the test."

Isaac remained mute as he climbed off the altar by himself. He was as astounded as a baby exiting the womb. Indeed, Isaac felt as if he had died and was now reborn.

His father went on, "Long ago, God chose me to spread His word throughout the world, but God still needed to test my faith. Now that I have passed this test—no—now that *we* have passed this test, God's blessing, as well as the land of Canaan, will pass to you, my son."

His father hugged Isaac, but Isaac kept his hands at his sides as if they were still bound. While his father was secure in his faith, Isaac was shaky in his. His head overflowed with questions. His heart was bursting with a jumble of emotions. Isaac needed to be away from his father, to be by himself, so he headed down the other side of the mountain alone.

As he picked his way through the brush, Isaac addressed himself. "I tried to make him stop, but he wouldn't hear me. He was going to kill me. My father was going to kill his only son. If this is the faith needed to do God's work, perhaps I am the wrong vessel. I don't know, maybe such faith is too dangerous. I don't know."

Isaac looked up to the sky and announced, "Rather than lifting me, the blessing weighs heavy like a curse."

Isaac's body and mind continued stumbling down the mountain until a clear vision of his mother appeared to him and helped ease his way. As he walked on, Isaac realized that his mother was dead. But while her body was no more, Isaac knew that her spirit would be with him for as long as he lived. At this thought, Isaac raised the corners of his mouth, turned south, and began the long journey home.

The
Trickster
Transformed

*T*here must be a way to teach them right from wrong," God said.

"What about that scroll You wrote?" asked Gabriella, God's chief angel. "You know, the Bible. Won't that do it?"

"The Bible's pretty good, but there are lots of illiterates down there. Besides, times change. Already it needs a few revisions. I don't have the time."

"Have you thought about appointing a few humans as teachers?"

"Quality control," answered God.

"Hmm, You have a point. I've heard some of the 'wisdom' from those claiming a direct link with You."

"If there was only a way to ... I've got it!" God yelled. God's face lit up like an exploding supernova. "I'll put a chunk of Divine Spirit inside every human to guide them through life."

Gabriella scratched her halo.

"If they have such easy access to the Divine Spirit, they'll have no choice but to always do the right thing. What about free will?"

God absentmindedly tossed shooting stars across the sky. "What if I give them tiny pieces of Divine Spirit? That way it will only help and not overpower them."

"I don't know."

"Okay, what if I hide it deep in their souls? That way they'll find it only when they really need it."

Gabriella nodded and God smiled.

●　●　●

Jacob and his twin brother, Esau, wrestled inside their mother's womb for nine months. When it was time to be born, Esau shoved Jacob aside and headed through the birth canal. Jacob grabbed Esau's heel to yank him back, but no luck; Esau emerged first.

As they grew up, the brothers followed separate paths. Esau loved the outdoors and became an expert hunter. While Esau was a man of the field, Jacob preferred to stay in camp. Their father, Isaac, loved venison, so Esau was his favored son. Rebecca, their mother, preferred Jacob.

One day Jacob was cooking a pot of red lentil stew. As he was stirring the pot, Esau returned from an unsuccessful hunt. He had been away for four days and was famished. He trudged over to Jacob and pointed at the pot.

"Give me some of that red stuff. I'm starving."

Jacob clucked his tongue at his brother's bad manners. Nevertheless, he was about to ladle a bowl for Esau, but he stopped himself.

"You know," Jacob thought to himself, "Since Esau was born first, he gets the birthright. But he really doesn't need it. All he needs to be happy is a bow and a couple of arrows. I, on the other hand, would make good use of the birthright. Maybe I should trade with him."

A tiny voice no louder than Jacob's beating heart interrupted his thoughts. "Who are you kidding? That's no trade, that's stealing—a clear violation of the Seventh Commandment."

"Huh?" Jacob said.

"Come on, brother," said Esau. "What are you waiting for? I'm starving."

Jacob stared at his brother.

"A trade. My lentils for your ... birthright."

"My birthright? You want my birthright?" Esau stared back at Jacob. He needed to eat or else he would die. Jacob had him.

Esau laughed. "Okay, brother. You want it that badly, eh? Take it. It won't do me any good if I'm dead."

Esau took the ladle and filled a bowl. He looked up from his lentils to see Jacob with a self-satisfied smile on his face.

"Brother," Esau said, "You'll get yours, you trickster. Mark my words. You'll get yours."

Up in heaven, God wondered if it would have been smarter to put a slightly larger bit of Divine Spirit into the humans.

Isaac's eyesight dimmed; he thought it was a signal that death was approaching. It was time to bless one of his sons and make him the clan leader. Esau, his firstborn, was a man of ability and action. He would make a fine leader. He called him into his tent.

"Esau," he said, "Go hunt me something, and I will give you my blessing when you return."

Esau picked up his bow and walked out of the tent, nearly knocking over his mother who had been standing outside, listening.

"A disaster," Rebecca said to herself as her eyes followed Esau heading into the desert. "A leader has to be smart with his head, not his hands. A leader has to have a vision of what can be, not just of what is. The clan needs Jacob."

Rebecca hurried to her favorite.

"Jacob, go get me a young goat from the flock. I'll prepare it for your father, and then you pretend to be Esau and receive his blessing."

Jacob smiled at his mother. Yet, as he ran to the flock, that tiny whisper again popped into his head.

"Don't do it. The Torah commands, 'Do not place a stumbling block before the blind.' "

Jacob quickly looked around for the source of the voice. He didn't see anybody, but he did stub his toe on a small rock.

Jacob muttered to himself, "Better a moment of dishonesty than an eternity of a dunce leading the Hebrew people."

"If it is meant for you to lead the clan, it will happen without sacrificing your integrity."

Jacob ignored the voice and brought a goat for his mother to prepare. Rebecca gave Jacob some clothes that Esau stored in her tent. To finish off the disguise, Rebecca placed pieces of goat skin on Jacob's smooth arms to emulate Esau's hairy skin.

"What about my voice?" Jacob asked.

"Pretend you have a cold," Rebecca advised.

When Jacob entered Isaac's tent he found his father lying on his bed.

"Father (cough, cough)," said Jacob.

Isaac turned his ear to the open tent flap.

"Which of my sons are you?"

"(Cough) It is I, Esau (cough), your firstborn."

Sounds like Jacob faking a cold.

"Sit up and (cough, cough) eat my game that you may give me your innermost (cough) blessing."

"How were you able to succeed so quickly, my son?"

"God (cough) granted me good luck."

God? When did Esau ever mention God?

"Come close, my son, so I may feel you and see if you really are Esau."

Jacob came close and Isaac ran his hands up and down Jacob's arms.

Goatskins. Is this a trick?

"Are you really Esau?"

"I am," said Jacob.

"Then let me eat your food."

Jacob served Isaac.

Definitely goat. Exactly how Rebecca makes it.

"Come close and kiss me, my son."

Jacob kissed Isaac.

Esau's clothes, but clean. This man has not been hunting. Add it all up and it's Jacob standing before me.

"I will wait for you to (cough) finish your meal."

Jacob slowly chewed some goat.

So that's the plan. You want the blessing. Clever. Very clever. No one could accuse you of being thick. Of course, Rebecca's behind this.

"Some (cough) drink, father?"

Jacob handed Isaac a cup of wine.

Hmm, maybe Jacob is the right one. He's smart and he really wants it. He might make the better leader. I love Esau, but he's not the sharpest arrow in the quiver.

A small voice popped into Isaac's head.

"Not sharp? You think hunting is easy? Clearly you never tried outsmarting an antelope. Jacob is destined for greatness, but don't reward him for deception."

Isaac took a deep draft of wine. Though he loved Esau more than Jacob, and despite that strange little voice, Isaac decided to give his blessing to Jacob.

Up in heaven, God remarked to Gabriella, "Like son, like father."

"I don't think Your Divine Spirit idea is working too well," she replied.

Back on earth, Esau returned home and discovered that he had been duped. Esau picked up his bow, refilled his quiver, and bellowed, "I'm going to kill that trickster!"

Rebecca had anticipated Esau's reaction, so as soon as Jacob left Isaac's tent, she had sent him on the road faster than one can say, "Hear, O Israel, Adonai is our God, Adonai is one."

As Jacob hiked under the blazing desert sun, he heard the voice, now a bit louder, "So, Jacob, where did your deceit get you?"

Jacob stopped.

"Who are you? Where are you? What are you?"

"You'd rationalize killing your own father, if it got you what you wanted."

"Leave me alone," Jacob said and trudged on.

The wilderness stretched from horizon to horizon. Jacob kept walking until the sun set and then looked for a place to stop.

"Here is as good as anywhere," he said addressing a small thornbush.

Jacob moved a few sticks and laid his cloak down as a bed.

"What a joke," Jacob said to a passing owl. "This morning blessed by my father. Tonight I've got a rock for a pillow."

He lay down and muttered, "Maybe I should start listening to that voice."

Jacob fell asleep and dreamed the most vivid dream of his life. Usually the voice of the Divine Spirit that gives life and truth to dreams gets garbled in the midst of civilization. Alone in the wilderness, the Divine Spirit came to Jacob clearer than his mother's voice.

A ladder stood with its feet on the ground, its top in heaven. Angelic beings climbed up and down the ladder. The ones coming down flew off in different directions. The ones going up disappeared into a large cloud. After watching for a few moments, the cloud lit up as if on fire, and Jacob averted his eyes from the bright light.

Then out of the fire came the voice. No longer tiny, it boomed.

"Don't worry, Jacob," said the voice. "I am God and I will be with you wherever you go. I will bring you back to this land, for it is for you and your descendants."

"If You do all that," Jacob said, "then You can be my God."

Gabriella clucked her tongue and said to God, "And if You don't do all that, You wouldn't be his God? Please."

God nodded. "Give him time. He's still young and thinks the world is quid pro quo."

Jacob awoke and sat up. The ladder and the dream were gone.

"I had no idea that God could be here in the middle of nowhere."

Gabriella remarked to God, "Most of them don't realize that You're everywhere. Everywhere a human opens his heart, there You are."

God looked into the future and replied. "It's funny how many of them will think they can only get in touch with Me through synagogues, temples, churches, and mosques."

● ◗ ◗

Jacob continued on his way, leaving his homeland behind. He settled with his uncle Laban and for seven years took care of his uncle's sheep and goats in order to marry his beautiful cousin Rachel. On their wedding night, Laban tricked Jacob by bringing Leah, his less attractive eldest daughter, to Jacob's tent. In the morning, Jacob realized that he had married Leah and needed to work seven more years for Rachel.

"What goes around comes around," said Gabriella.

Besides being in charge of Laban's huge flocks, Jacob was provider for his two wives, two concubines, eleven sons, and one daughter. There simply was no time for God; he was too busy to hear the Divine voice.

When Jacob grew older, he turned over most of the shepherding duties to his sons and found himself with a day to himself. Jacob went to a nearby creek and rested beneath a fig tree growing by the bank. Jacob listened to the babbling brook, the soft wind blowing through the tree, the birds singing, and that distinct voice he had heard so long ago.

"It's good to relax," the voice said, "but when are you going back to Canaan? It's yours, remember?"

"If I go back," Jacob said, "Esau will kill me."

"If I were him, I'd be thinking the same. But it's you, not him, who is destined to lead the clan and father a nation. Don't be bothered by the thought of Esau thrusting a sword into your belly."

Jacob felt queasy in the stomach.

"Listen," God added, "I promised I'd bring you back safe and sound."

"You don't know my brother. He's ruthless."

"I'm God, for God's sake. I'm not exactly powerless."

The tree's figs suddenly all dropped and covered Jacob in sticky ooze.

"Fine, I'll go."

So Jacob took his wives, concubines, sons, daughter, goats, camels, sheep, donkeys, and cattle and set off for his homeland. When he came to the border of Canaan, he sent messengers to Esau.

"Return to your master," Esau told the messengers.

The messengers mounted their asses and rode off.

Esau lifted his bow high above his head and screamed, "To the death of my brother!"

Four hundred armed men lifted their weapons and roared, "Death to Jacob!"

"Yes, my faithful," Esau continued, "after twenty years, vengeance will be mine!"

Again the men roared. Esau smiled from his rock perch. A murmur rose from the rear of the ranks. Men parted and an elderly couple made their way toward Esau. The woman wore a tan jilbab embroidered with black thread at the neck, wrists, and hem. She wore a gold necklace, gold earrings, and a gold nose ring. Her gold bracelets clanged as she walked. The woman walked unafraid, her eyes defiant. In contrast to the woman was a stooped man, his white jilbab stained at the neck. Cataracts clouded both his eyes with an opaque blue-white film. He leaned on the woman and appeared lost.

The couple stopped before Esau's rock and looked up at the warrior chief. It had been many years since Esau last saw this man and woman, his father and mother. Esau signaled his men to help them up the rock. Esau's parents stood only three feet away from him, but he greeted them with a voice loud enough for his men to hear.

"Mother, I should have expected you, but Father, this is a surprise. You are well?"

"Praise the Lord, my son, we are well," said Isaac.

Esau nodded, looking not at his father, but at his mother. His lips pursed, he raised his eyebrows slightly.

"Esau," she began and stopped. In a softer voice, "Esau, my son. You know why we have come."

The corners of Esau's mouth turned up.

"Indeed. I may not be as brilliant, or should I say as cunning, as my brother, but I understand. Oh, I understand. You came for the trickster's life."

A shout erupted from the men, "Death to Jacob!"

Esau held up his hand and silenced them.

"Dear Mother and Father, perhaps you have forgotten? I haven't. Though the injuries happened a generation ago, the wounds are as fresh as yesterday's."

Esau turned to his men.

"Come close and hear what happened before most of you were born.

"I, Esau, am the firstborn child of Isaac and Rebecca, who stand before you. I was hunting, for my father loves the taste of game. It was an unlucky hunt. I went for four days but found nothing. My food stocks were empty. Yet, for the honor of pleasing my father, I ignored hunger, until my strength failed. I was out for too long and took ill. I needed to eat, or I would die."

Esau paused.

"On my way home, I came upon my brother preparing a pot of lentil stew. I said, 'Brother, I'm starving. Give me some stew.'

"If I live to be as old as the gods, I'll never forget the smile that came across his face, the smile of victory, the smile of 'I got you.'

"'Of course, brother,' he said. 'Take all you desire. Only first a trade. Your birthright for the stew.'"

Esau faced his parents.

"Father, have you ever known hunger? Mother, have you ever faced death?"

Esau turned back to his men.

"I had no choice. I agreed. I agreed to the scheming plan of my trickster brother. I sold him my birthright for a bowl of lentils."

"That was a long time ago, my son," said Rebecca.

"Besides, what good has the birthright done Jacob? He has been a fugitive for twenty years, while you've got four hundred men."

"Time does not heal injustice. Only justice heals injustice. And who are you to lecture me? You planned the deceit that cost me Father's blessing. Do you not remember?

"'Bring me the game that I love,' Father said to me, 'and I'll give you my blessing.'

"So dutiful Esau carried out his father's command, while his mother planned his downfall.

"Don't play shocked, Mother. I know it all.

"'Go fetch a goat, Jacob,' you said, 'and I'll make it how your father likes. Here are Esau's clothes. We'll fool him and he'll bless you.'"

"Esau, my son," said Isaac, "your mother did what she thought best."

Esau stared at Isaac.

"What Mother thought best?" roared Esau. "No, what *Father* thought best. It was you, Father. You abandoned your firstborn, the son you loved. You knew. How could you not? You're not as stupid as you let on."

"Esau," Rebecca said sharply. "Honor thy father."

"Mother, I do not honor deceit."

Esau lifted his bow high above his head and shouted, "I honor justice!"

The men yelled, and Rebecca led Isaac home.

◦ ◌ ◦

When Jacob's messengers returned with a report of Esau's four hundred men, he prayed.

"Oh, God. You told me to return to my land and You would protect me. I am not worthy of all that You have done for me these past twenty years. When I left Canaan, I had only my cloak. Now because of you I am a wealthy man. Save me from the hand of Esau, for I am afraid."

Up in heaven Gabriella turned to God.

"Aren't You going to say anything to him?"

"Now? No."

Down below Jacob waited for a reply.

"Has God abandoned me?" he whispered to himself.

Jacob's eldest son, Reuben, interrupted Jacob's prayer.

"Father, what would you have us do?"

Jacob took one last look to heaven, sighed, and commanded that two hundred female goats, twenty billy goats, two hundred ewes, twenty rams, thirty camels, forty cows, ten bulls, twenty asses, and ten foals be sent to Esau. He instructed Reuben to send the animals in four waves.

"Surely this is more than the birthright was worth," said Jacob. "I hope it satisfies him."

That evening Jacob sat alone on the bank of the Jabbok River. The gurgling water calmed him. For the first time in weeks, thoughts of Esau left his head, and his body relaxed. Jacob closed his eyes, and with each long breath, Jacob felt himself expand until he could not separate himself from either the universe or God.

Jacob sat in this state of oneness until a man kicked him.

"What's going on?" the startled Jacob yelled, but the man had already sprung on him. Jacob slipped out of the man's grip and faced his adversary.

"C'mon," said the man, "show me what you have."

Jacob knew the voice. It was familiar, but he could not place it.

"I don't know your grudge against me," said Jacob, "but you won't prevail."

The two wrestled all night until dawn's first light approached. Jacob had the man pinned, and the man struggled to get away. Jacob held on tighter. The man twisted and wrenched

Jacob's thigh. Jacob screamed but did not let go.

"Let Me go!" the man cried.

"Let you go?! You started this. Bless me before I let you free."

"Very well."

Jacob released his grasp. The man stood up and Jacob stared at him. After fighting all night, the man had not a mark on his body.

"Tell Me your name," the man said.

"Jacob."

"No longer will you be called Jacob, but Israel—for you have wrestled both God and men and have won."

"What are you talking about?"

"Israel means 'he who wrestles God.' "

"Who are you?"

"Don't ask My name. You know who I am."

The man vanished. Jacob groggily stood up, as if waking from a dream. A sharp pain tore through his thigh, and Jacob fell over. His staff lay next to him. He used it to lever himself up. Jacob surveyed the area. It looked as if someone had been rolling around. A sharp rock protruded from the dirt. Jacob's cloak was covered in dirt; his thigh was black and blue.

Jacob limped across the river and suddenly recognized the voice.

"Oh, my God!" he said to himself as he struggled to gain footing on the opposite bank of the river. "But why wrestle me?"

●   ◯   ●

Esau saw shepherds driving livestock toward him and his army. Esau stopped a shepherd.

"Whose flocks are these?"

"They belong to your servant Jacob. They are a present to his lord Esau."

"Never!" exclaimed Esau. "To think I can be bribed with fifty sheep. I've been waiting twenty years for this day."

"Forward!" he called to his army.

Minutes later Esau encountered a second flock.

"What, more?" said Esau.

The shepherds bowed.

"These flocks will make me far richer than I ever dreamed," Esau said after receiving the fourth and final flock. "Still the arrogant rat doesn't deserve to live."

- - -

"What happened, Father?" Reuben asked when Israel limped into camp.

"You are no longer the children of Jacob. You are the children of Israel, the wrestler of God."

Israel's face glowed. His sons stepped back.

Israel's youngest son, Joseph, pointed at Israel's leg. "Was that a sacrifice?"

Israel smiled. His young son spoke the wisdom of youth. One does not receive something for nothing. There is a cost, a sacrifice, for everything good.

"Yes, my son. It was a sacrifice."

Joseph ran into Israel's arms. "Father, I am afraid Esau will kill us."

Israel stroked his favorite son's black curls. "Don't be frightened. I've wrestled God. What can Esau do to me?"

Israel was deaf to the pleas of his elder sons and servants who wanted to fight. Israel instructed his children and servants to remain behind, while he alone went to face Esau's army.

"Oh, God," prayed Israel, "I need You. Don't forsake me. I'm the one who kindled Esau's anger. Let me be the one to quench the flame. I don't want to die, but if I must, let it be quick."

"You are doing right," the crystal clear voice told Israel.

Esau watched a limping man hobble forth from Israel's camp.

"Look at that pathetic emissary," laughed Esau. "The trickster is trying to appeal for sympathy."

Fire flashed from his eyes.

"I will destroy his army of cripples."

When the limping man came closer, Esau recognized his brother.

"It is not an emissary, but your humbled brother reaching out to you," a distinct voice spoke from inside Esau's head.

"Jacob?" Esau muttered under his breath.

"Hug him," the voice continued.

Esau stared hard at his limping brother. With his bow in his hand, he raced hard toward Israel.

"Hug him," the voice called to Israel, and Israel quickened his shuffle.

The two brothers faced each other. Israel dropped his staff and Esau threw down his bow. The brothers embraced. The Divine Spirit flowed from one to the other. God and the entire universe smiled as, for a brief moment, peace was made on Earth.

Joseph's School

Israel was an old man with twelve sons. A wise man would have spread his love evenly among his children. Israel, however, showered all his love on Joseph, his eleventh son, the first child of Rachel, his favorite wife.

While his older sons tended his flocks, Israel excused Joseph from work. He provided Joseph with tutors who taught the boy to read and write, play musical instruments, figure sums, and speak foreign languages. In addition to spending his days enlarging his mind, Joseph loved to beautify himself with expensive oils and lotions.

Day by day, as Joseph's knowledge and beauty grew, his soul remained small. By the time Joseph turned seventeen, the age of adulthood, he was still only a child.

Israel loved Joseph, but Joseph's ten older brothers did not. They resented the spoiled brat who never lifted a finger to help. They rolled their eyes at his oiled hair. They were jealous that women found him handsome. They despised him for being a tattler.

One day Joseph was walking through the fields playing the flute when he came upon his brother Gad killing a lamb. Joseph ran home to tell his father how Gad was squandering the family fortune. When confronted by Israel, Gad lied, explaining that a lion had attacked the flock and crippled a lamb before he could run it off. Gad told his father that he was simply putting the lamb out of its misery when Joseph showed up.

Israel forgave Gad, but the brothers did not forgive their brother, the fink. Always thinking the world revolved around him, Joseph was oblivious to the venomous looks his brothers shot him every day.

● ● ●

"Your ways are a mystery to me," said Gabriella, God's chief angel.

"Sometimes they're even a mystery to Me." God grinned.

"I mean, I thought this clan was Your chosen people."

"They are."

"So why send them to Egypt into slavery?"

"You temper a knife by plunging the blacksmith's red hot blade into water."

"Sometimes it cracks," Gabriella said.

"Sometimes it doesn't," God replied.

"And what's with the brat? This kid who cares only about new sandals is going to lead them?"

"He's a little soft," God agreed. "He needs to see the big picture."

So God sent Joseph two dreams.

In the first dream, Joseph and his brothers were binding wheat sheaves in the field, when Joseph's sheaf stood up. Surrounding and bowing down to his sheaf were his brothers' sheaves.

Joseph woke up and told his brothers the dream.

And the brothers hated Joseph even more.

A few nights later Joseph dreamed again. This time the sun, the moon, and eleven stars bowed down before him. Again Joseph related the dream to his family without omitting a detail.

And the brothers hated Joseph even more.

Israel, too, was blind to the brothers' hatred of Joseph. He assumed that the rest of the world loved Joseph as much as he did.

He never imagined that when he gave Joseph the most colorful coat in all the land, the brothers' thoughts would turn murderous.

"The spoiled brat makes me sick," began Shimon.

"Look at my coat," said Zebulon. "Issachar handed it down to me. He got it from Asher, who got it from Gad, who got it from Naphtali, who got it from Dan, who got it from Judah, who got it from Levi, who got it from Shimon, who got it from Reuben."

The brothers looked at Zebulon's ratty jacket. It resembled a spider's web more than a piece of clothing.

Then Gad gave voice to the thought that was on all their minds.

"Let's kill Joseph and be done with the dreamer."

The brothers' eyes gleamed in assent.

● ◍ ◍

Israel did not completely trust his sons with the flocks. One day he sent Joseph to spy on the brothers.

"Don't forget to take your coat," Israel told Joseph. "It's chilly in the hills."

Joseph headed in the direction his brothers had gone, but he got lost.

"This kid couldn't find a palm tree at an oasis," Gabriella said.

"He needs a little help," said God. "Would you mind?"

"Whatever," she groused.

The chief angel ditched her halo and wings, dressed herself as a man, and found Joseph tracking his own footprints in the sand.

"What are you looking for?" Gabriella asked in a husky voice.

"For my brothers."

"You won't find them here. I heard them say, 'Let's go to Dothan.' That's on the other side of those hills."

Joseph thanked the man and headed to the hills. As he walked, three questions popped into his mind about the man. First, how did that guy know he was looking for something? Second, how could he be in a position to overhear the brothers discuss where they were going? Third, how did the man know that the brothers were *his* brothers?

Joseph shrugged his shoulders.

"Probably it was an angel," he said.

Joseph had no more time to think on the matter because he soon came upon his brothers.

• ⬭ •

Shimon saw him first. "Look at that. It's the little rat."

Zebulon leaned on his shepherd's crook. "The rat and his coat."

Gad drew his knife from its scabbard. "Let's see what becomes of his dreams."

Reuben held Gad's arm. "No, brother. We don't want blood on our hands. Let's just throw him into that pit over there."

The other brothers nodded, and Gad put his knife away.

"Hello, brothers," said Joseph. "How is my father's flock?"

"Your father's flock is fine," said Gad.

"Uh, good," said Joseph, looking quizzically at Gad, who was smiling at him for the first time since Joseph could remember.

"Have you come to help shepherd the flock, brother prince?" asked Asher.

"No. Father sent me to ..."

"Check up on us?" interrupted Shimon.

"What a fine son you are," said Zebulon, taking hold of Joseph's arm. "Come, brother. I'll show you the newborns. But, I must warn you. The sheep are very dusty. Allow me to take your coat. We wouldn't want it to get dirty."

"It's a little chilly. I think I'll keep it on."

"I insist," said Zebulon, who with the help of Gad and Shimon, stripped the coat from Joseph's back.

"Give it back, brothers!"

"Give it back, brothers!" mocked Shimon.

The brothers lifted the screaming Joseph off the ground.

"Put me down! I'm serious! This isn't funny! You're really in trouble! I'm telling Father!"

The brothers dropped Joseph into the pit.

"Help! There's a snake in here! I'm not kidding! Let me out!"

Gad peered over the edge. "You said we'd bow down to you. Now look where you are. So much for your dreams."

"Father's going to punish you, all of you! A scorpion's on my sandal! Get me out!"

"I'm hungry," said Levi. "Let's eat."

The ten brothers sat down next to the pit and started eating. On the horizon, Shimon spied a caravan of traders.

Judah said, "Brothers, what do we gain by letting Joseph die? Sure, he's a despicable little rat, but he's our brother. Why not sell him?"

The brothers nodded, pulled Joseph out of the pit, and sold him for twenty pieces of silver.

Zebulon tried on Joseph's coat. "What do you think?"

Asher laughed. "Oil your hair, shave your face, take a bath, and make yourself less ugly, then you're sure to get some girls."

The brothers took the coat and slaughtered a goat. They dipped the coat into the goat's blood and returned home to show it to their father, who mourned the death of his beloved son, eaten by a lion.

Gabriella looked down and said, "Israel fooled his father with a goat, and now he is fooled by his sons with a goat. Now that's what I call poetic justice."

God grinned. "Is this a great creation, or what?"

● ◗ ◐

"I demand that you release me!" Joseph yelled.

"Shut up, slave!"

Joseph stopped and faced the speaker.

"I am not a slave. I am the son of Jacob, messenger of God. Send word to my father. He will pay you handsomely for my return."

A fist crashed into Joseph's face. Joseph fell into the sand. Rough hands lifted Joseph back to his feet; blood trickled from the corner of his mouth.

"Shut your mouth and get moving."

Joseph shuffled along on shackled feet. He had never realized that his brothers hated him. Clearly they were jealous. After all, he thought, I'm smarter, better looking, and father's favorite.

As Joseph trudged along under the broiling sun, he mumbled one more thought, "They've got nothing to be jealous of now."

● ◗ ◐

When the traders came to Egypt, they sold Joseph to an Egyptian named Potiphar. Joseph quickly learned to avoid Potiphar's whip by making sure Potiphar got what he wanted even before Potiphar himself knew what he wanted. Before the summer sun was high in the sky, Joseph had a cool drink ready for his master. On his own initiative, Joseph organized the other slaves to dig an irrigation canal. After the canal was in, Potiphar's crops were no longer dependent on the yearly flooding of the Nile.

Not only was Joseph spared the whip, but, for the first time in his life, Joseph felt useful to someone other than himself. His soul began to grow.

Potiphar's new slave made him rich. To reward Joseph, Potiphar put him in charge of his house. With his new position, Joseph's life eased; soon he was back to oiling his hair and wearing beautiful clothes. Joseph spent more and more time in front of the mirror, and less and less time on his work.

"Still a little Narcissus in him," said God.

"Nothing a little more suffering couldn't cure," Gabriella suggested.

● ⬤ ◍

Joseph was naturally good-looking, but when he made himself up, women dropped their pots and stared. For Potiphar's wife, Zuleika, Joseph's presence was absolute torture. She lusted after her husband's favorite slave. She tried thinking of other things, but the harder she tried to turn her thoughts from Joseph, the stronger grew her desire for him. Whenever she saw him, her body quivered. She had to have him, for that which is denied is the seed of desire.

One day while Potiphar was away on business, Zuleika ordered all the slaves out of the house. When Joseph came to serve her lunch, she greeted him in an evening gown.

"Put the tray down, Joseph. I'm hungry for something else. Come to my bedroom."

Zuleika was a beautiful woman. Joseph, as if in a dream, followed his master's wife to the bedroom.

"Sit next to me," Zuleika commanded, patting the bed. Joseph sat and Zuleika removed Joseph's coat from his back. The touch of her hands awakened Joseph to the sin he was

73

committing, and he jumped up and raced from the room.

"Come back!" Zuleika yelled, Joseph's coat in her hand.

"That slave has made a mockery of me," Zuleika said to herself. "If I can't have him, nobody can."

Zuleika opened her window and cried for help. The other slaves came running. "The Hebrew slave tried to rape me. Here is his coat, which he left behind."

When Potiphar heard what had happened, he whipped Joseph and then sent him to prison.

God said to Gabriella, "Sometimes they need to go down in order to come up."

"Funny creature You created," said Gabriella.

God nodded.

●　◍　●

For the first two days in prison, Joseph stood in his five-by-three-cubit cell screaming, "She lied! I didn't touch her! She tried to seduce me!"

Outside the cell the guards spoke to each other.

"I know just how he feels. Last week Zuleika wanted me."

The guards laughed, opened a small slot at the bottom of the stone door, and shoved in Joseph's daily ration—watery leek soup and moldy barley bread.

"Here, lover boy. Compliments of your girlfriend."

After screaming himself hoarse, Joseph wrapped himself in a flea-infested blanket and sat on the cold dirt floor, feeling neither fleas nor cold, only bitterness. Bitterness at Zuleika. Bitterness at Potiphar. Bitterness at his brothers. Bitterness at God. For a full year, bitterness was Joseph's only companion. Yet, bitterness neither satisfies nor heals. It lies on the soul like a heavy coat, so one day Joseph stopped blaming everyone else and turned inward. It seemed to Joseph that his life was layered with coats. It took prison for Joseph to begin peeling the layers away.

"It doesn't take a genius to see why Potiphar abandoned me," he said to the wall. "Though I was the honorable one, it was my word against hers. But was it my fault she pressed herself on me?

"I always thought it was a blessing to be handsome. Maybe it isn't. Maybe a little modesty would be good. Maybe I need to think how I make others feel.

"A good lesson to learn."

Joseph then strapped himself into his brothers' sandals. His brothers were the ones who worked and kept the family prosperous, yet it was Joseph whom Israel had showered with gifts. For the first time, Joseph saw himself clearly, the brat who flaunted his father's favoritism in front of them all.

And then the dreams.

"Stupid and idiotic. That's what I was. Telling them they were going to bow down to me. What was I thinking? I'm lucky they didn't kill me. If I ever see them again, I'll apologize, and maybe they'll forgive me."

Joseph touched one of the prison walls and chuckled at the irony. It took the physical restrictions of prison to free his soul. After resolving his bitter feelings toward the people in his life, he turned to God.

"It is You who led me down into this dark dungeon in order that I may realize my true self. From this moment on, I dedicate myself to You. All that I do will be for Your glory."

"A little melodramatic, don't You think?" Gabriella commented to God.

"It's only because you're cynical," God said.

Joseph did not try to convert his fellow prisoners and jailers to his God. Instead, he tried to make prison life more tolerable for all. In Potiphar's house, Joseph had learned the art of cooking. Since both jailers and prisoners despised the rotten prison food, Joseph offered to cook. So pleased were they by his culinary talent, the jailers put Joseph in charge of all the prisoners.

Two new prisoners arrived, Pharaoh's baker and cupbearer. A pebble had found its way into Pharaoh's bread, causing him to chip a tooth. That was why the baker was in chains. The cupbearer had been was imprisoned because Pharaoh discovered a fly in his wine.

Soon after they arrived, they each had a confounding dream.

Joseph said, "Tell me your dreams. Surely God can interpret them."

The cupbearer went first. "On the vine were three branches of grapes. I took the grapes, pressed them into Pharaoh's cup, and placed the cup in Pharaoh's hand."

Joseph replied, "Pharaoh realizes that it was not your fault a fly flew into his wine after you placed it before him. You will be restored to your former position in three days. But when all is well with you, think of me and mention me to Pharaoh. In truth, I was kidnapped from the land of the Hebrews and am truly innocent."

Next came the baker. "There were three open baskets. In the top basket was food for Pharaoh. Birds were eating out of the basket."

Joseph replied, "You should have been more careful in checking your dough for pebbles. In three days Pharaoh will put your head on a pole, and the birds will pick off your flesh."

On the third day both of Joseph's interpretations came true. But the cupbearer forgot about Joseph. And though by now Joseph was an adult in both age and spirit, he remained imprisoned two additional years before Pharaoh released him.

"Now it's even," God said to Gabriella upon Joseph's release from prison. "Seventeen years as a brat, seventeen years as a slave, and now those dreams I gave him will come true. Joseph will make everything ready for when the Hebrews go down to Egypt."

Gabriella nodded. "Oh, I get it. You're going to put the whole tribe through what Joseph went through."

God nodded.

"Isn't there an easier way?" the angel asked.

"I wish there was."

Moses

God's
Stutterer

en Hebrew slaves groaned as they pushed a huge stone block up a steep incline. Small-diameter tree trunks jammed under the rock worked as rollers. A thick rope was tied around the two-ton mass. Thirty slaves pulled on the rope, while whips cracked on the backs of those who slipped. Cubit by cubit the block ascended the ramp. No one noticed the fraying rope until there was a loud pop, and the stone rolled backward. Two men were immediately crushed to death. All the others, except one, jumped out of the way. A teenage boy stumbled, and the rock rolled over his legs. The other slaves raced to his aid.

"Stop!" the Egyptian overseer commanded, veins bulging from his contorted face. "Get another rope and get back to work!"

No one moved.

The overseer grabbed the nearest slave by the throat. "You have until the count of three, and then I break his neck!"

The slaves retreated. The overseer shoved his hostage away and knelt next to the screaming youth.

"Two crushed legs," he said. "Bad luck. You can't work no more."

The overseer slid his knife from its sheath and plunged the blade into the boy's heart. With his last breath, the Hebrew sent forth a scream that pierced the heavens.

God and Gabriella were taking a meteor shower when they heard the scream.

"What was that?" God exclaimed.

"What was what?" asked Gabriella.

"That scream."

"Oh, *that*. I'm sure it's nothing."

"Nothing?" said God. "Let me take a look."

God pointed a telescope toward Egypt. After a moment God thrust the telescope into Gabriella's hands.

"You call *that* nothing?" demanded God.

Gabriella looked. "I call it nothing new. Humans. You were expecting—what, compassion?"

Gabriella put down the telescope and looked God in the eye. She saw God's pain and sadness. No doubt about it, God suffered with the oppressed. No arguing on this one. Another nice evening ruined. Gabriella sighed, opened her notebook, and said, "Okay, what do I do?"

"Find Me a human who can lead these slaves to freedom."

Gabriella spoke as she wrote, "Find ... human ... leader." Gabriella scratched her head and asked, "What do You need a human for? I'll do it myself. I'll make a humongous earthquake. In the confusion, I'll split a sea and the slaves can escape. Easy as genetic modification."

God smiled the smile of one about to checkmate an opponent.

"Look, if we do it for them, where's their feeling of accomplishment? Their self-esteem? Of course we'll help, but I don't say 'I help those who help themselves' for nothing. Now go. Have a nice visit."

Gabriella slammed her notebook closed. "Have a nice

visit. Have you forgotten how much I hate mixing with this species? It's common knowledge that they're one of the cruelest creatures in Creation. Besides, I can't stand the way they stare at my wings."

"You do have nice wings," God said and toweled off the meteors.

* ◉ *

Two women sat across a table from each other. One held a papyrus scroll in her hand.

"I can't believe it," said Shifra, after reading Pharaoh's decree that they, the midwives, must kill all male Hebrew babies. "This is one paranoid guy."

"Your basic male," answered Puah, Shifra's midwife partner. "Thinks he's a god. But I see where he's coming from. Let's say Assyria attacks Egypt. Whose side do you think the Hebrews are going to fight on?"

"I don't care," said Shifra. "I'm not killing any babies."

Puah nodded. "Sometimes you just have to take a stand."

When Pharaoh discovered that the midwives were not following his orders, he summoned them to his throne room.

Now Pharaoh did indeed think of himself as a god, and his throne room reflected his lofty view of himself. Tiny windows on the ceiling let light stream in, mimicking the sun's rays breaking through the clouds. Music filled the giant room with ethereal, otherworldly sounds. All of Pharaoh's personal items—from his crown to his chamber pot—were fashioned from pure gold. He was surrounded by warriors and advisors gripping swords and quills at the ready. Food was ubiquitous, though only Pharaoh ate.

The midwives were hustled in and left stranded before the elevated throne. Pharaoh, who could create anxiety in a rock, made the two women stand there while he finished his meal. He ate delicately and slowly. After licking his fingers clean, he picked up a gold file and manicured his nails. Halfway through his second hand, he stopped to admire his handiwork, and asked in a nonchalant voice, "Why did you let the Hebrew boys live?"

Shifra did what any fast-thinking person does when found out by the power of a despot—she lied. She gave Pharaoh a story about how Hebrew women were not like Egyptian women. They were more like animals. When they felt contractions, they just squatted wherever they were and gave birth. By the time the midwives appeared, the women and babies were gone. There was nothing to be done.

Pharaoh grunted and dismissed them with a flick of his wrist. After they left, Pharaoh called his advisors.

"Well?" he asked.

His first advisor said, "Maybe it's the truth and maybe it's not. I propose that we torture the midwives and find out."

His second advisor said, "Maybe it's the truth and maybe it's not. I propose that we follow the midwives and see what they do."

Pharaoh shook his head. "Maybe it's the truth and maybe it's not, but it doesn't matter. The midwives don't matter," he said with a smile. "I have a better idea. Let the parents do the deed. Make a decree that all baby Hebrew boys are to be thrown into the river. Any person caught with a baby boy is to be executed on the spot."

Pharaoh turned his attention to a golden goblet of wine. "Dismissed."

The next day the decree was posted.

○ ◌ ○

A Hebrew woman gave birth to a beautiful boy. For three months she hid him, until he was too big to conceal any longer.

The woman knew that she had no other choice but to put him into the river the following day. That night she and her daughter Miriam cried themselves to sleep. When the sun rose, Miriam told her mother the dream from which she had just awakened. In Miriam's dream, her mother had put the baby in a basket and left it among the reeds at the river's edge, at the spot where Pharaoh's daughter came for her daily bath. The childless princess found the basket and took the baby for her own.

Up in heaven God chuckled. "Now *that's* a brainstorm." Gabriella had earlier complained that there was not a single leader to be found among the Hebrews. God concurred and planted the dream. "Imagine, a Hebrew in Pharaoh's family. Pharaoh himself will teach him the skills he'll need to lead the Hebrews from slavery. I love irony."

The child's mother put the boy in a basket and placed it among the reeds. Miriam watched. Pharaoh's daughter came and found the basket. When the princess opened it, she found a crying baby.

"This is one of the Hebrew children," she said. She held the baby and soothed him until he quieted. "I never knew that babies felt so warm and soft."

Miriam jumped from her hiding spot and surprised the princess. "Do you want me to find a Hebrew wet nurse to suckle the child for you?"

Pharaoh's daughter hardened her face and glared at Miriam. In the commanding voice of royalty she demanded, "What are you doing at my private spot? Why aren't you at work, slave?"

Miriam was caught. Now not only would the baby be killed, but she would be, too.

"Well, slave? Speak!"

Sweat beaded on Miriam's forehead. She opened her mouth, but nothing came out. Pharaoh's daughter stared at

Miriam, then at the baby, and then back to Miriam. The corners of her mouth lifted and her dull eyes brightened.

"Go, fetch me the nurse."

The princess held the child close and said, "I drew you out of water, so I will call you Moses, which means 'he who draws out.' I pray to the gods that you will fulfill your name and draw out wisdom and power. For when you become Pharaoh, you will need plenty of both to rule well."

Moses's mother came to the princess, and for two years she nursed him. While he suckled, she softly sang Hebrew songs. When the time came for Moses to be weaned, his mother whispered into his ear, "Moses, remember this: You are a Hebrew. Never forget." Then while biting her lip to keep from crying, she handed the little boy to the princess.

Raised in Pharaoh's household, Moses joined the most privileged class in the world. Indulged in the niceties of life, educated by the best minds in the kingdom, and taught by his adoptive mother that he had a special destiny, Moses became the Prince of Egypt.

While Moses was nurtured to rule, he had been born with a defect that helped shape who he would become. For a reason God only knew, the link between his brain and mouth was weak, giving the prince a severe stutter.

In outsiders, disabilities evoke pity. Yet, in Moses's case, his was a blessing. His stutter prevented him from catching arrogance, the princely disease. His speech humbled him and he learned empathy, something previously unheard of in Pharaoh's court. Empathy gave Moses the desire to ease the suffering of others.

Prince Moses enjoyed lingering among the Hebrew slaves. As he made his rounds about the kingdom, their strange language attracted him. When Moses was upset, only their music could soothe him. In the deep oceans of his mind, Moses believed he was not Egyptian, but a Hebrew. The surface waters, however, rarely speak with the deep oceans, and, for the most part, Moses saw himself as the Egyptian prince that he was raised to be.

● ● ●

The suffering of the Hebrews increased. They cried to God, and God decided it was time to free the slaves. God commanded Gabriella to check on Moses. Gabriella found the prince observing an Egyptian overseer beating the life out of a slave. Moses took out his sword, looked to the right and to the left, and killed the overseer. The Egyptian turned to see who had the audacity to murder him. There was Moses, Prince of Egypt, holding a bloody sword in his hand. The overseer looked at him quizzically before crumpling to the ground. The Hebrew ran away. Moses returned the sword to its scabbard and hid the Egyptian in the sand.

Good, thought Gabriella, this guy stands up for justice and is a man of action. Okay, maybe killing the overseer was a bit over the top, but what can you expect; he is Pharaoh's grandson. Gabriella waited for Moses's adrenaline level to decline. News that you've been singled out by God is always better taken sitting down. While waiting, Gabriella witnessed a second scene. One Hebrew was beating up another slave.

Moses stepped between the two men and said, "W-w-why are you ... h-h-hitting your ... n-n-neighbor?"

The first Hebrew turned on Moses, "Who made you ruler over us? You going to kill me like you killed that Egyptian?"

Moses froze. His secret was out. If Pharaoh finds out, thought Moses, he'll kill me.

Without waiting another moment, Moses fled Egypt.

Gabriella kicked the dirt at her feet and started a dust-storm, her job not finished. Moses was definitely the one, but he was not ready to lead. First of all, the Hebrews did not accept him as their leader. And, more important, he didn't stick out a tricky situation.

Gabriella sighed, adjusted her halo, and flew after the flee-ing prince.

● ⬤ ●

Moses did not stop running until he arrived at an oasis in Midian. He sat down, removed the sandals from his aching feet, and thought about everything that had happened. He kept replaying the incidents over and over in his head, thinking how he would do things differently if given another chance.

His chance came soon enough.

As Moses massaged his feet, seven sisters were filling the water troughs for their sheep. A group of shepherds came and cru-elly drove the girls away. Moses wanted to do something, but he was outnumbered. The shepherds could easily kill him if he made trouble. But Moses could not just sit idly by. He gulped down his fear and called to the shepherds, "W-w-why … d-d-drive off the … g-g-girls? There's enough … w-w-water for everyone."

"L-l-listen, s-s-stranger," mocked one of the shepherds, "keep your nose out of where it don't belong. I'd hate to mess up your fancy clothes with your own blood."

The other shepherds laughed and moved menacingly close to Moses.

"Stay out of this," a second shepherd said. "These are the daughters of Jethro, the priest of Midian. These are his sheep. He preaches that there's only one god. What a load of crap. His sheep don't deserve no water."

"B-b-but," persisted Moses, "do ... sh-sh-sheep care what we ... b-b-believe? They're just ... th-th-thirsty. May I ... h-h-help water ... th-th-them and they will be ... q-q-quickly out of your ... w-w-way?"

The first shepherd stared at Moses and laughed. "Sure. Why not." To his friends he said, "This ought to be good, an Egyptian nobleman watering Jethro's sheep. L-l-let's ... w-w-watch."

God and Gabriella watched, too.

"Backbone!" exclaimed God. "And compassion! And smarts, too. That's it. He's ready."

"Great. I'll tell him, and I can finally finish this wretched assignment."

God held her wings. "Not so fast, my angel. We can always contact Moses. But he needs to figure out how to get in touch with Me. He has to discover the doorway."

"Discover the doorway!" Gabriella protested. "But that could take years! I have a life, You know."

"Patience, Gabriella," God said. "Anyway, you could learn something from this Moses."

● ● ●

While Gabriella waited, Moses married Jethro's eldest daughter, Zipporah. Soon he became a father and took over his father-in-law's flock. As it turned out, Moses enjoyed being a shepherd much more than being a prince. No people to boss around, no affairs to go to, and, best of all, no speeches to make. Moses fell in love with the desert solitude. What Moses most loved about the desert was that time was measured by the seasons, not by the hourglass that ran his life as a prince. Unshackled from the stress of being a busy Egyptian nobleman, Moses was able to enjoy God's creation. The seasons passed and he put his former life behind him.

One day Moses was pasturing the flock at the far edge of the wilderness near Mount Horeb, the mountain of God. He had little on his mind as he walked. At one point, he watched an eagle soar from one side of the horizon to the other. The bird gave Moses a feeling of peace, a feeling of completeness, as if he and the desert were one. Moses inhaled deeply as his eyes came to rest on a small bush. Something about that bush made him pause. It was just an ordinary plant: He saw hundreds like it every day. Yet, this one looked different. Moses stopped and stared. The bush burned with a strange light. It was as if the bush were on fire, yet the flame was still strong long after the bush should have been burned up. Moses did not understand it at the time, but he was seeing beyond the surface of the plant and viewing its life force, its divine spark, the gateway to heaven.

Moses was knocking on God's door, and God was there to answer.

"Moses, Moses," God said.

"H-h-here ... I-I-I am," Moses replied.

"Don't come closer. This is holy ground. Take off your sandals."

The bush burned brighter. Moses shielded his eyes as he removed his sandals.

"I'm God," said God. "I've seen the troubles of the Hebrew people and have heard their cries. I've come down to rescue them, bring them out of Egypt, and take them to a good land. I'm sending you to Pharaoh; you will lead them out of Egypt."

"Y-Y-You're ... j-j-joking," stammered Moses.

The bush burned even brighter.

Moses reached for his sandals. "Y-Y-You have the wrong ... g-g-guy. Who am I to go before ... Ph-Ph-Pharaoh and bring the ... H-H-Hebrews out of ... E-E-Egypt? I'm a ... sh-sh-shepherd, not a ... p-p-prophet."

The bush glowed bright orange.

"B-b-besides, the … H-H-Hebrews hate … m-m-me."

The bush continued to burn.

"They won't … b-b-believe me and they won't … f-f-follow me."

The bush still burned.

"F-f-for the sake of … a-a-argument. S-s-say that I … g-g-go. The … p-p-people are … g-g-going to … w-w-want to know the … n-n-name of … G-G-God. What … w-w-would I … s-s-say is Your … n-n-name?"

"I will be that which I will be," said God.

"W-w-what?"

"Tell them that the God of Abraham, Sarah, Isaac, Rebecca, Jacob, Leah, and Rachel will bring them out of slavery," said God.

Moses finished putting on his sandals. "W-w-why don't … Y-Y-You tell … th-th-them, b-b-because they will … s-s-say, 'G-G-God has … n-n-not appeared to y-y-you.'"

God said, "Throw your staff on the ground."

Moses did and the staff turned into a snake. Moses jumped back.

"Now pick it up," commanded God.

Moses looked as if he had just been asked to jump off the top of a pyramid.

"Go on. It won't hurt you."

Moses grabbed the viper by the tail and it turned back into his staff.

God said, "If they don't believe you, throw the staff. They'll believe, believe Me. But, if that doesn't work, try this."

God instructed Moses to put his hand inside his shirt and draw it back out. Moses did so. His hand had turned white with leprosy. He repeated the procedure and was healed.

"One more?" said God. "Take some water from the river.

The Triumph of Eve

Pour it on the land. The water will turn to blood. If they still don't believe you, they stay slaves. Any questions?"

"I'm slow of … s-s-speech and slow of … t-t-tongue," said Moses.

"Listen, if I can speak from inside a bush, you can make yourself heard with stutter. Besides, I'll be with you. If it will make it any easier, take your brother Aaron with you. He's a talker. Just tell him what to say. Deal?"

"D-d-do I have a … ch-ch-choice?"

God thought for a moment. "Do you?"

Moses thought about his quiet life, his loving wife, his beautiful children, his sheep, and his desert. The idea of returning to Egypt to lead a slave rebellion was at the top of his never-in-a-million-years list. Yet, despite the years of his peaceful shepherd life, the images of Hebrew slaves screaming, crying, and dying had never completely left him.

Moses looked deeply into the bush, sighed, and said, "D-d-deal."

The
Argument

When Jonah was first given a glimpse into the future, he thought nothing of it. Two weeks prior to his sister giving birth, Jonah dreamed the baby would be a girl. Jonah told the dream to his brother-in-law, who chuckled, because he dreamed she was having a boy. When a baby girl was born, it was Jonah's turn to laugh.

Next time it was in the middle of a summer heat wave, when Jonah dreamed of a child sledding down the snowy hills of Jerusalem. When he awoke, he smiled at his preposterous dream. Three days later when a child sledded by him during a freak snowstorm, Jonah began to wonder.

By the time Baruch's wife told Jonah that Baruch was missing, Jonah knew that Adonai, the Israelite God, had blessed him with the gift of seeing into the unknown. A few nights earlier, Jonah had dreamed that Baruch fell into a well. Jonah organized a search party and found Baruch in the well that he had dreamed of.

After finding Baruch, Jonah began going to sleep earlier. The more sleep, he thought, the more prophetic dreams. Soon, however, Jonah tried avoiding sleep altogether as the future of the Israelite nation was revealed to him. Jonah foresaw a time when his country's poor would be ignored. He foresaw the destruction of Israel's forests and the barrenness that would follow. He foresaw the Hebrew people abandoning Adonai.

Then came the worst dream of all. In this vision, Jonah

foresaw the annihilation of ten of Israel's twelve tribes at the hands of Assyria, their hostile neighbor to the north.

Every time Jonah awoke from this nightmare, his nightgown dripped with sweat. Even as he sat upright in bed, he could still hear the cries of hungry children and widows. The smell of burning villages remained in his nose long after he arose. Images of princes bound in chains were indelibly etched into his mind.

Perhaps the worst part was that Jonah had no one to tell. In Israel the economy was good and the people were happy. If he were to prophesy destruction, people would laugh and call him mad. Jonah knew that people only see disaster once the sword tip pricks their flesh. Of course, by that time, it is too late.

Then one morning everything changed and Jonah was happy again. The nightmares about Israel's destruction gave way to a wonderful dream where the evil people of Assyria were annihilated instead. With Assyria gone, Israel would live. Jonah jumped out of bed and danced through the streets. His burden was lifted and stayed off his shoulders until the day God came to him with a request.

God is the most mysterious force in the universe. There have always been those who seek to experience and understand God. God, however, is elusive and difficult to find. Occasionally, a person may be granted a vision of God. Sometimes the vision is blissful. Sometimes the visionary experiences pure terror when confronting the awesome power of God. When Jonah met God face to face, the only emotion he felt was anger.

"You want me to prophesy in Nineveh, the capital of Assyria?" Jonah repeated, unable to believe his ears. "But I thought You were going to destroy them. They're evil."

"And Israel is perfect?" asked God.

"Oh, come on. That's not fair. We're not perfect, but the Ninevites, the Ninevites are wicked and rotten. Everyone knows that they deserve to be wiped out."

"You're right," said God. "At the very least they deserve a good plague. But I want to give them a second chance. Who knows? Maybe they'll repent, and I'll relent."

"What happened to justice?" asked Jonah. "What's more, if You don't destroy them, they're going to destroy Israel."

"I wouldn't be so sure," said God. "The future isn't chiseled in stone."

"You mean the Assyrians won't destroy Israel?"

"I mean, nothing is preordained."

"Well, that's not good enough for me. Find someone else to save those sinners."

With that, Jonah grabbed his bedroll, and, instead of heading up to Nineveh, he went down to the port city of Jaffa, where he bought passage on a boat going to Tarshish.

"Tarshish," said Jonah with a smile. "The other side of the world. Let the God of Israel find me there."

Jonah went down into the ship's hold and laid out his bedroll.

"With that God out of my life, I can finally get a decent night's sleep," he said to himself.

By the time the ship left Jaffa and headed down toward Tarshish, a sleep as deep as death had overtaken the prophet.

● ◖◗ ●

"Quaint," said Gabriella, God's right-hand angel. "The human believes he can escape from You."

"Backbone," said God. "He's got backbone. Did you see him stand up to Me? Whenever the rest of them see Me, they grovel, snivel, and beg. Doesn't make for satisfying relationships."

"You call it backbone. I call it stiff-necked pigheadedness. Let me find someone else who would be happy to prophesy to the Ninevites without a big to-do."

"Nope, Jonah's the one. The only problem is, I've got to make him see things My way. That's your job."

Gabriella sighed. "If I weren't immortal, You'd be the death of me."

Gabriella glided down from heaven. The other boats on the Mediterranean Sea soon beheld a strange sight. While they sailed in tranquil waters, a small, yet violent thunderstorm pelted a single ship.

The sailors on that particular vessel lashed down everything as the boat tipped back and forth like a broken balance. Jonah slept through the rocking. Sailors threw cargo overboard to lighten the load, while water poured into the boat. Jonah slept through the flooding. Soon the ship began to sink. The captain ran below deck to see if there was anything else that could be tossed overboard. In the darkness of the hold, he stepped on something soft.

"Ugh," said Jonah.

"What's this?" yelled the captain. "The storm's blowin' like the devil, me sailors are doin' everythin' to keep from sinkin', and here you're stretched out like a corpse! Get up, man! Call to your god!"

"My god is Adonai, God of the land of Israel, not god of the sea."

"I don't care who your god is! Up to the deck!"

The captain pushed Jonah up to the deck. The sailors were huddled around the first mate. He held divining lots in his hand.

"Come, men," said the first mate. "We all know that this here ain't a regular storm. Some god's mad. Take a lot and see who's to blame."

Jonah and the sailors picked, and the lot fell on Jonah.

Jonah stared at his lot. The sailors stepped away from him.

"Who are you?" demanded the captain. "And who is Adonai?"

Jonah looked out at the churning waters. Adonai was much, *much* bigger than he had imagined. He turned and faced the sailors.

"Who am I?" said Jonah. He again examined the lot in his hand. "I am Jonah. Who is Adonai? There is only one God, the God of everything, Adonai."

"What have you done?" the sailors asked.

"I fled from Adonai."

"How can we calm Adonai?"

Jonah now understood the impossibility of fleeing from God. Yet, there was no way he was going to prophesy to Nineveh. Sometimes principle is more important than life.

"Throw me overboard," said Jonah. "That should satisfy Adonai."

"I ain't killin' no prophet," said the captain, and he commanded the sailors to go to their oars. They rowed hard toward land. Gabriella, however, sent a gusting headwind that blew the boat farther out to sea.

The men cried to God, "Please, Adonai, don't make us guilty because of this man, but we ain't got no choice."

The sailors took Jonah and lowered him over the side until his feet touched water. The storm suddenly ceased. The sailors pulled Jonah back up, and the storm returned full force. They lowered Jonah to his waist. Again the storm stopped, and again the sailors pulled him up. The storm came back stronger. They lowered Jonah to his chin. The storm subsided. They pulled him back up and the storm raged.

"Well, mates," said the captain. "Ain't nothin' else to be done." The sailors let go of Jonah, and he sank under the waves.

God, however, was not going to let Jonah drown. As Jonah fumed about the unfairness of it all, he sensed the presence of a large object nearby. He turned to face the open maw of an extremely large fish.

"As if drowning weren't bad enough," the prophet gurgled to himself.

Jonah was sucked into the mouth of the fish. He was pressed and squeezed through the fish's muscular throat into its dark, cavernous belly. At first, Jonah thought he must be dead. Yet, if he were dead, why was he pinching his nostrils to avoid smelling the decaying muck he was sitting in? No, he may have wished he were dead, but he was very much alive, sitting in the pitch black of the fish's belly, sinking deeper and deeper into despair.

After three days, Jonah could take it no longer. He cried out, "God, you win! Get me out of here!"

Immediately, the fish rose from the depths and spat Jonah out onto dry land. The exhausted prophet fell onto his hands and knees. Before he had a chance to brush off the seaweed and fish entrails, God appeared to Jonah.

"Nineveh?" moaned Jonah.

"Nineveh," said God. "Go up and speak to that great city."

Jonah got up and headed up toward Nineveh.

God turned to Gabriella, "See? It took a little persuasion, but he got it."

Jonah, however, got something completely different. During the three days inside the fish, Jonah came to realize that in the history of the Israelites, they never listened to Adonai's prophets. If the Israelites didn't believe, how much more so would the wicked Ninevites ignore a prophet, especially one smelling like old, rotting fish? Jonah smiled. He would have the last laugh on God.

Unfortunately for Jonah, the adage "Man plans and God laughs" was as true then as it is now.

Jonah strode into Nineveh's busiest open-air market. Shoppers gave him wide berth.

Excellent, thought the pungent prophet. Jonah stopped in

the market's pastry section, stacked a couple of empty crates, stood on his rickety pulpit, and announced, "Sinners of Nineveh!"

Always eager for diversion, the shoppers smiled and stopped to listen.

Jonah raised his hand until all was quiet. He then shouted, "In forty days Nineveh shall be overturned!"

Jonah stepped down and quickly walked out of the market, saying to himself with a smile, "Well, that's that."

Disappointed that the madman had not been cleverer, the shoppers picked up their bags. Before they dispersed, however, a voice boomed, "Wait!"

A sailor ran through the crowd and leapt on top of Jonah's crates.

"That man is a prophet of Adonai, the true God!" the sailor proclaimed.

"Go back to sea!" the crowd yelled.

"Please, good people, listen," the sailor implored. He was joined by other sailors. "We sailed from Jaffa and that man was on board. Because of him Adonai sent a storm that almost sank us."

"It's true," said a second sailor.

"We almost drowned," said a third.

"When he went overboard, the storm stopped," the first sailor said.

"It's true," said the second sailor.

"We didn't drown," said the third.

"Listen to his words," said the first. "He speaks the truth."

For a moment the market was quiet, as the shoppers digested the sailors' words. They looked for Jonah, but he was gone. A vegetable vendor climbed up on his table.

"O, God, Adonai! Forgive me and don't kill me. My balances are fixed. To all the people I've cheated, come, I'll make it up to you."

Suddenly, everyone began apologizing to one another.

One man jumped onto Jonah's crates and proclaimed, "Let everyone fast and pray! Perhaps if we turn from our evil ways, Adonai will forgive us!"

"Yes! Yes!" the people cried, and the Ninevites turned from their evil ways.

● ● ●

God found Jonah lingering outside the city.

"Good job, Jonah," said God. "The Ninevites repented and I'm going to let them live."

Jonah was incredulous. "You can't! It's not fair! It's not just! This is why I fled in the first place. You're too merciful, and I don't want any part of this. Take my life because I'd rather die than live."

"You're upset about Nineveh?"

"So upset I want to die."

God, however, did not strike Jonah down. Instead, Jonah sat on a hill overlooking Nineveh. The second that the Ninevites reverted to their old ways, Jonah was going to let God know. Then he would watch the city burn in fire and brimstone.

The day was hot, so Jonah built a shade hut. Unfortunately, to his great discomfort, the sun still beat hard on his head. The next morning, God grew a plant to shade Jonah. Jonah was happy because now he could sit comfortably, while he waited for Nineveh's fall.

God, however, had plans other than Jonah's comfort.

The next morning, God sent a worm to kill the plant. Then God sent a hot wind along with a scorching sun to beat down on Jonah. Jonah grew faint and begged, "Take my life because I'd rather die than live."

"You're upset about the plant?" God asked.

"So upset I want to die."

"And you're still mad about Nineveh?"

"I don't think it's too much for the Judge of the Universe to deal justly and give people what they deserve. The Ninevites only changed because they are afraid You're going to kill them. They're still evil. You know that."

"Listen, Jonah," God said. "Everybody makes mistakes. Sometimes even Me. What about mercy? Where does that fit in?"

"As far as I'm concerned, it doesn't."

"So you deserved the shade from the plant I provided?"

Jonah did not answer.

"And you were so upset when I took it away that you now want to die?"

Jonah said nothing.

"Understand this, Jonah. I didn't need to create the world. Justice didn't compel Me to do it. I created the world to allow mercy to grow."

Jonah got up and left. He figured that it was no use arguing with God, even when he knew that God was wrong. Jonah returned to Israel, and God did not destroy Nineveh.

●　◗　●

In 722 B.C.E., 123 years after Jonah's death, the descendants of the Ninevites whom Jonah had saved invaded Israel and annihilated ten of Israel's twelve tribes.

Uncorked
Perfume

More wine!" roared King Ahasuerus from his throne.
"But Your Majesty ..." began the king's cupbearer.
Ahasuerus lifted the cupbearer by his lapels and belched his fiery breath into the trembling man's face.

"More ... wine ... now!"

The king released the cupbearer, who stumbled backward into Prime Minister Haman.

"Oh, good Haman," the cupbearer pleaded. "The king has been drinking nonstop for three days. I fear for his health. Please talk to him. He listens to you."

Haman adjusted his three-pointed hat and replied, "His Majesty has suffered terribly since he banished the queen. It will not harm him to temporarily find solace in alcohol." Haman turned to watch Ahasuerus throw his empty goblet at the musicians. Under his breath the prime minister muttered, "Of course, even if the queen still reigned, that fool would be drunk by this time of night." To the cupbearer he advised, "Dilute the king's wine with water. He will not notice."

The cupbearer bowed to the floor. "Oh, thank you, thank you, good Haman. Your advice is sound, as always."

Haman smiled and tipped his hat. He was brilliant, wasn't he? After all, wasn't he the one who planned the coup that brought that oaf Ahasuerus to power?

"Drink, you drunk," said Haman as the smiling Ahasuerus

was served an overflowing goblet. "It doesn't matter if you're sober or drunk. Just keep doing as I tell you, and your kingdom will be fine."

Haman removed his hat and brushed off the dandruff before returning it to his head.

"Who would ever have thought that I, Haman, the scrawny kid that everyone beat up, would one day have power over all their lives? *I don't want Haman on my team. He's a geek. You take him.* That's what one team captain said. The other replied, *Over my dead body.*"

Haman smiled at the memory. Both captains were now dead bodies, hanged by Haman's command. Then there was the pretty girl who had rejected Haman's invitation to dance. She didn't say a word. Just laughed in his face. She was now a broken, stooped-over chambermaid, thanks to Haman. Everyone who ever hurt or crossed Haman met similar fates.

"Yes, power is good."

Ahasuerus spilled wine on his royal robe.

"I better find him a new queen to keep him busy. If he has too much time on his hands, he might start acting like a king."

The next morning Haman ordered a beauty contest to find Ahasuerus a new queen.

● ━ ●

"Haman makes my wings curl," Gabriella confided to God.

"Nice guy he's not," God agreed. "Why don't you fly down and …"

"Definitely not!" interrupted Gabriella. "It's time for us to stay out of human affairs. How are they ever going to grow up if You always bail them out?"

God put a hand on Gabriella's shoulder and said, "When you're right, you're right. And you're right."

Gabriella smiled. It wasn't every day that she got her way with the Omniscient Force of the Universe.

"Just do Me one favor," God said. "Make Ahasuerus take a liking to long-haired brunettes."

Before Gabriella could utter a protest, God left to design some organisms for God's next creation. In her pocket Gabriella found a sheet of parchment titled, "Small Errands, Really Nothing at All."

The angel groaned, tucked the To Do list into her robe, and flew down to Earth.

●　◗◗◗　●

"… 498, 499, 500," said the beautiful young maiden. She set her brush on the table and gazed at her face in the mirror.

"Hadassah!" her uncle Mordechai yelled from the next room. "Are you going to stare at yourself all day? Let's go!"

Hadassah came out of her room and walked past her uncle. "How can you spend hours a day in front of your mirror?"

Hadassah turned and faced her uncle. "How can you spend hours a day in front of your 'holy' books?"

"You equate the study of God's holy words to painting your eyes?"

Hadassah did not reply, but, like Mordechai, she did not believe that their daily activities were equal. Unlike her uncle, she believed hers were superior. Even as a child, Hadassah understood the power of beauty and realized that she could wield it over men. When she walked into a room, heads turned and mouths dropped. Men vied for her attention by telling her the stupidest nonsense. They never cared what was inside her head or her heart. She could have been a murderer; it would not have mattered to them. They just wanted to own the beautiful girl and have bragging rights.

Hadassah, however, did not want to be a wife. She wanted more out of life than making babies and cleaning house. Yet, as a woman, Hadassah had no power to be anything but some man's property. Her only hope of escaping a life of dirty diapers was in the power of her beauty.

"Come on, Hadassah. Let's not be late again."

"Relax," she said. "It's not like we've got an audience before the king. We're going to synagogue. Big deal."

"It *is* a big deal," corrected Mordechai. "At synagogue you are standing before the King of Kings. I wish you would dress more modestly, like the other girls."

The two walked out into the street.

"Uncle, if you think I want to be like the other girls, you have it wrong. I am not about to marry some guy and spend my life sewing clothes for a dozen kids."

"I have it wrong? No, my niece, you have it wrong. There is no higher calling than raising children. Listen, Hadassah, I'm not blind. A pretty girl should expect to marry a handsome boy. That is only right. I'll find you a suitable match."

"Whatever."

Hadassah and Mordechai made way for the king's soldiers, who were marching down the street. Hadassah smiled at the captain, who, when he turned to look at Hadassah, marched into a tree. Mordechai sighed. He had to get his beautiful black-haired niece married fast, or she would marry out of the faith, diminishing the Jewish people even more.

"What's this?" Hadassah exclaimed as the wind blew a handbill into her face.

Hear ye! Hear ye! Hear ye!
A Proclamation from our
Noble, Wise, Rich, Powerful, and Handsome

King Ahasuerus.

He Desireth a Bride.

All young maidens of Enchanting Beauty are invited
to enter the
King's Beauty Pageant
From which the New Queen shall be chosen.

"Disgusting," grumbled Mordechai. "Our pagan king is the
shallowest of men. Is it not written, 'A beautiful bottle can conceal bad wine'?"

"Does not God desire beauty? Does not the Torah require
that sacrifices to God be flawless and pleasing to the eye?"

"Are you debating Torah with me?" Mordechai demanded.

"I am only saying that I am entering the pageant," said
Hadassah.

"Marry a pagan?" said Mordechai. "I forbid you!"

"Look, Uncle," said Hadassah. "I'm not abandoning
Judaism, but if we always stay in our shtetl, only marry our own,
how will the people of the world learn about God? After all,
what good is a precious perfume if it's stoppered in its flask?"

"Hah!" said Mordechai. "More likely, you would become
pagan."

"I would not."

Mordechai stared at his niece and began to think that the
beauty pageant might not be such a bad idea. Hadassah was
pretty, but she had no chance of winning. Thousands of girls
from the far reaches of the kingdom would be competing. After
losing, Hadassah might finally come to her senses and marry a
nice Jewish boy. Perhaps, if Mordechai were lucky, a scholar.

"All right," he said. "Go. I give you my blessing. Just one
thing. Don't use your real name. I'll lose face if my friends find out.
Call yourself Esther. It means 'secret.' It will be our little secret."

Hadassah—er—Esther hugged her uncle and went to prepare for the pageant.

The next day Esther joined a huge harem of girls vying to become Mrs. Persia. Esther graded her competition one by one.

"Hair too stringy; bad rouge; ugly; bad posture; tiny butt; ugly dress; big butt …," and so on and so forth.

Esther felt confident until she met the real competition. The first was a dark-skinned beauty with an hourglass figure; her green eyes were flawless emeralds; her hair, polished cascades of ebony. She moved with the elegance of the Queen of Sheba. The second girl was tall and light-skinned with shapely legs that seemed to go on forever. She had a face that would make Aphrodite jealous and a mane of silken mahogany that fell to her waist. Her deep blue eyes reminded Esther of sapphires.

"You three," a eunuch called, motioning Esther and the two other beauties. The three were brought before the king.

"They are all so lovely," Ahasuerus said. "Can't I have all three?"

"Of course, Your Majesty," said Haman. "But I suggest you choose only one to be queen."

While Esther was not more beautiful than either of the others, she alone knew how to wield her beauty as a tool. Esther tilted her head down slightly, locked her fetching eyes onto the king's, and the Persian empire had its first Jewish queen.

Not only did Esther conceal her true name from the king, but she kept her Jewish identity a secret as well. For seventeen years she had lived by Jewish law. Eat this, don't eat that. No cooking on Shabbat. Fast on Yom Kippur and so on and so forth. Esther was tired of the rigidity. The palace court was filled with all kinds of delicious foods, and, with the exception of pork, Esther partook of everything. Even though she no longer kept kosher, the thought of eating pig made her queasy.

Esther always believed that she was destined for greatness.

Now as Queen of Persia, her dream had come true.

● ◗ ●

"Since taking his new wife, Ahasuerus no longer eats pork," Bigthan whispered to Teresh outside the city gates.

Teresh, who co-owned with Bigthan the largest pig farm in the kingdom, nodded his head and whispered back, "There are whispers that the new queen is a secret Jew."

"If she has her way, pork consumption will plummet! She'll put us out of business!"

"Let's kill the king and find one who won't let a woman talk him out of ham."

"Right. But how?"

"Arsenic in his wine?"

"Perfect."

The two men shook hands and left. A third man sitting in the shadows of the gate overheard the plot. It was Mordechai. Earlier he had been sent an unsigned note to hide at the city gates. After the two plotters left, Mordechai went straight to Hadassah, who reported the matter. By the morning's first light, Bigthan and Teresh were hanging from gallows.

On a cloud overlooking the city, Gabriella took out her To Do list and crossed out:

Send Mordechai note to hide at city gates Tuesday night 10:00 p.m.

● ◗ ●

One morning, Prime Minister Haman was strolling through the capital city, Shushan. Wherever Haman passed, the people bowed; it was the law. Haman walked by the city gate and all the elders bowed, save one, Mordechai.

"Bow, you idiot!" a friend hissed. "Haman can make you wish you were dead."

"I bow only to God," he replied. "I would rather die than bow down to a mortal."

"You're about to get your wish."

When Haman passed by, Mordechai remained standing, so Haman stopped. His assistants stepped back.

"What is your name, insolent one?" Haman said, pointing at Mordechai.

"I am Mordechai the Jew."

"Jew? Did you say Jew? You Jews think you're better than us, above our laws, don't you?"

"With all due respect, honorable prime minister," Mordechai began, "we are loyal citizens ..."

"Insolence! You dare contradict me! Haman snapped his fingers and an assistant appeared at his elbow. "Write this one's name in my black book," he said. To Mordechai he sneered, "We shall see you soon, Jew."

As Haman continued his walk, a devious idea came into his head.

The Jews are rich. If I can do away with them, *I'll* get their money, and I won't need Ahasuerus anymore. King Haman. Now there's a royal name that's pronounceable.

The next morning Haman strode straight to the palace for his daily audience with the king.

"Your Majesty," Haman began, "there is a certain foreign people scattered throughout your kingdom that have their own laws and ignore yours. I fear that if an enemy appears at your gates, this people will turn against you."

Ahasuerus jumped up and exclaimed, "We must do something!"

Haman smiled. "Your Majesty's prime minister has not been sleeping. Please, Your Majesty, sit."

Ahasuerus sat.

"All has been made ready. All that is needed is your approval. If it pleases Your Majesty, let an edict for their destruction be drawn up."

The king removed the signet ring from his finger and handed it to Haman. The deal was sealed.

Up in heaven, Gabriella clicked her tongue. "So human. Pretending to do something good in order to cover the tracks of your evil."

Daniel, the angel of justice, nodded. "I never take the word of a human seriously."

God gave it a different spin. "They conceal from each other that which they conceal from themselves."

● ⬭ ●

When Mordechai read the edict that the Jews were to be annihilated on the thirteenth day of the month of Adar, he exchanged his clothes for sackcloth. He spread ash over his face, arms, and legs, and cried bitterly throughout the city until he came to the palace.

"Your Majesty," one of Esther's maids addressed her. "A man wearing sackcloth and in need of a bath is calling for you. He claims to be your uncle Mordechai. Shall I instruct the guards to send him away?"

What could have happened to him? Esther wondered. Was he swindled out of his money, or had he given too much to the synagogue?

Esther sent him a change of clothes. Mordechai sent them back, so Esther went to the palace gate.

"Uncle, what's the problem? Do you need money?" Esther opened her purse of gold and silver coins. "Take what you need."

Mordechai showed her Haman's edict.

"You must go before Ahasuerus and try to stop it," Mordechai said. "You are our only hope."

Esther shook her head. "Sorry. I can't. One can only go before the king when summoned. That includes me. If I go without being asked, the penalty is death. Only if the king extends his golden scepter toward the person may she live. Mordechai, you have to understand, a person in my position cannot afford such a risk."

"Hadassah …"

"I am Esther."

"Esther, have you ever thought why you were made Queen of Persia? Perhaps it was for this moment."

Esther looked at her uncle covered in sackcloth and ashes, his back bent, his face begging. Wasn't *this* the reason she had fled her people? She was no longer Hadassah the Jew. She was Esther the Queen. She had risen to a position of wealth, fame, and power. Now she was being asked to risk it all, risk her very life to save the people she had escaped from. It was so unfair.

Mordechai interrupted her thoughts. "Every one of us is given a unique gift that no one else in the world possesses. One can either keep that gift to herself, or use it to benefit others. Esther, it is time to uncork your perfume."

Esther shook. The very words that she had spoken to Mordechai a lifetime ago. Esther felt the urge to look at herself and clawed through her purse for her hand mirror. She lifted the mirror and looked deeply into her perfect face. Was her beauty fair? Did she do anything to deserve her beauty? If she were to be truthful with herself, Esther knew the answer was no. Her beauty was a gift bestowed upon her at birth. A gift she must now use to serve others.

The queen addressed Mordechai. "Tell all the Jews to fast for three days on my behalf. I will do the same. Then I will go to the king. If I am to perish, then so be it."

"... 498, 499, 500. I am finished, Your Majesty."

Esther's maid held a mirror for her. Esther examined herself and asked, "How do I look?"

The maid replied, "I wish that I were King Ahasuerus to be wed to such a beauty as you."

Esther was ready. She strode across the palace grounds and came to the door of the inner court. Esther took a deep breath, smoothed down her royal robe, and forced a smile onto her face. She opened the door, and a guard announced, "Queen Esther."

King Ahasuerus looked up from his wine inventory and said in a severe voice, "I called you not."

Esther's stomach turned and an invisible noose tightened around her neck. "Breathe," she told herself.

"Well?" demanded the king. He was greatly displeased by this unwelcome intrusion.

Esther thought of all the innocent women and children whose lives depended on her.

Ahasuerus snapped his fingers. Two guards grabbed Esther's arms. Before returning to his wine list, his eyes met Esther's. There was something different about them, he thought. Their color hadn't changed, but they looked richer, deeper, determined. Esther knew the danger of coming uninvited, yet she was willing to risk her life for something.

A change came over Ahasuerus, and he realized that his beautiful Esther was a true queen. He raised his hand and the guards released Esther.

Ahasuerus extended his golden scepter. Esther walked across the courtyard to touch it.

"What troubles you, Queen Esther? And what is your

request? Even up to one-half of the kingdom is yours."

"If it pleases Your Majesty, please bring Haman with you to a feast that I have prepared."

"Your wish is gladly granted."

Later that same day, Haman passed by the city gates. Again Mordechai did not rise and bow, and Haman raged at his counselors.

"Build me a gallows! I am personally going to hang that Jew!"

Carpenters were summoned, and before the sun set, a new gallows was erected outside the palace gate.

• ◖ •

That night King Ahasuerus could not sleep.

"How much caffeine did you slip into his dessert wine?" God asked.

"Whatever was written on the list," Gabriella replied.

Ahasuerus rang the bell by his bed and called for his Book of Records to be read to him.

"If this doesn't put me to sleep, nothing will," he said.

Ahasuerus's servant opened the book. A light breeze came through the window, and the open book blew to a new page. Suddenly, the wind reversed direction, and the book blew back one page. The servant looked on with wide eyes.

God frowned at Gabriella. "I've told you a hundred times, no bending natural laws."

"Sorry," said the red-faced angel. "I overshot my mark."

"What are you staring at?" said Ahasuerus to the servant. "Read!"

The servant read the account of Mordechai denouncing Bigthan and Teresh.

"What honor did we bestow on this Mordechai?" asked the king.

"Nothing, Your Majesty."

"Nothing?" repeated Ahasuerus. "We must reward him. Any of my advisors about?"

It so happened that Haman was waiting outside in order to get the king's signature on the edict for Mordechai's hanging.

Haman entered the king's chamber, removed his hat with a flourish, bowed low, and said, "Your Majesty, thank you for seeing me at this late hour. I come to ask for a small request. There is a man ..."

"Haman," interrupted Ahasuerus, "what should be done for a man that the king wishes to honor?"

So, thought Haman, the cad is finally going to honor me. After all, the bum would still be a bouncer at the Good Grog Tavern, if it weren't for me. That Jew can wait.

"Your Majesty," began Haman, "let such a man be garbed in royal robes and be seated on your own horse. Let such a man be led throughout the city, and have proclaimed before him, 'This is what is done for the man whom the king desires to honor.'"

● ◗ ●

"Cheer up," said Haman's wife, after Haman had led Mordechai through the city on King Ahasuerus's horse. "Before long, revenge will be yours. Mordechai will hang with the rest of the Jews soon enough. As for you, tonight you have been invited to dine with King Ahasuerus and Queen Esther."

"You're right," said Haman. "Soon Mordechai and the Jews will be dead, and I'll overthrow the king."

"And I will become queen."

Haman smiled. He did not tell his wife that he was planning on keeping the beautiful Esther as his queen.

That evening Haman and Ahasuerus sat down to Esther's feast. The queen wore her power outfit—a low-cut, tight-fitting gown with a green bodice atop a long black skirt with a leg-revealing slit up one side. Both Haman and the king found it difficult to concentrate on their food, but drink they did. When Esther judged the men sufficiently drunk, she sat down next to the king.

Ahasuerus put his goblet down, placed his arm around Esther's waist, and pulled her close.

"You have made a magnificent feast, my queen. Now, tell me, what is your wish? Even to one-half of the kingdom, it shall be fulfilled."

Esther gingerly unwrapped the king's hand from her torso and stood up. "If it pleases Your Majesty, let my life and the lives of my people be granted as my wish, for we are to be murdered and exterminated."

Haman rose unsteadily, raised his goblet, and proclaimed, "I pledge my life to protect Queen Esther and her people."

Ahasuerus said, "Well spoken, good Haman!" Turning to Esther he said, "Who is the evil one who would commit such a crime against you and your people?"

Esther faced Haman and stared hard into his face.

"My Lord, I am a Jew."

A wave of nausea swept over the prime minister.

"My enemy is the evil Haman."

Haman cringed, and his hat fell off his head. Ahasuerus glared at him and stormed from the room. Esther sat on a couch and folded her arms. Haman knelt at her feet.

"Dearest queen," he said, "this is clearly a misunderstanding. I never meant you or your people harm. I love your people. It is only against those few who refuse to become part of our great kingdom—the ones who dwell apart from us and live by their own evil laws. They are the ones who threaten our security. You and your family have all proven your loyalty."

Esther was unmoved by Haman's words. Yet, Haman

knew that the game was not over. He might not be able to fool Esther, but he was confident that he could persuade Ahasuerus to see it his way.

Gabriella also knew it was a mistake to underestimate Haman as long as his head was still attached to his shoulders. Gabriella looked at her list. Nothing. She had to think fast. There was not a moment to lose. She invisibly ran behind Haman and shoved him onto the couch. Haman landed on Esther at the precise moment when Ahasuerus returned to the room.

"Do you mean to ravish Queen Esther in my own palace!" roared the king. "Guards!"

Two guards rushed in and grabbed Haman.

"Your Majesty," said Esther, "look out the window and you can see the gallows Haman constructed to hang Mordechai—the Jew who saved your life."

Ahasuerus looked out the window. "Your Jewish god is a just god." Turning back to the guards he commanded, "Hang Haman from the gallows that he meant for Mordechai."

●　●　●

Three months later, Esther was having tea with the new prime minister, Mordechai.

"Uncle, tell the truth. Wouldn't you agree that it was for the best that I married out of the faith? After all, if I were not queen, who would have stopped Haman?"

"I admit it. In this *one* case, it seems to have been for the best."

Mordechai took a sip of tea and placed his cup on the table.

"So, Hadassah ..."

"Esther."

"Esther," continued Mordechai, "now that you have saved

the Jewish people, what are your plans for the future?"

Esther smiled. "No plans except for taking care of this." She patted her pregnant belly.

"So you decided to be a mother after all."

"Why not? My maids will change the diapers."

"That's wonderful," said Mordechai. "Just one thing. You're going to raise the child Jewish, right?"

The Last Lesson

hree women, two young and one old, stared at two fresh graves. The young women sobbed and wiped away tears with the sleeves of their black dresses. The body of the older was slack, her face blank. While her lungs continued to move air in and out of her body, Naomi felt as dead as her buried sons. If the Earth would have exploded at that very moment, Naomi would not have noticed. Her world was already destroyed.

Twilight was approaching and Ruth, one of the young widows, lightly squeezed Naomi's shoulder. The other, Orpah, gently said, "Come, Mother, it is time to return home."

The word *home* roused Naomi from her stupor. She threw Ruth's hand from her shoulder and faced Orpah.

"Home?" Naomi mocked. "I am home. Here are my boys tucked in their beds, and there," Naomi pointed to another grave, "my husband sleeps peacefully. Thanks to God, my home is here."

"Naomi," Ruth said softly and again placed her hand on Naomi's shoulder.

Naomi stepped away from the touch.

"Don't! I will not be consoled." Naomi turned to address the setting sun. "What have I done to deserve this?"

An owl hooted in the distance, crickets chirped underfoot, the crimson heavens were silent.

"God is just," said Ruth. "It is not for us to understand God's mysterious ways."

"You who prayed to idols before I taught you about God. What do you know?"

Naomi clenched her fists. She wanted to hit someone, but the one she blamed had no form to strike. Instead, the tears started and her knees buckled. Ruth and Orpah caught their mother-in-law and helped her home.

The next morning, Ruth and Orpah returned from the well to find Naomi leading a packed donkey out of the village.

"Mother, where are you going?" Orpah asked.

"I came here to Moab ten years ago with a good husband and two fine boys. There is nothing more for this cursed land to take. I am returning back to Israel, to Bethlehem."

Naomi clucked her tongue, and she and the donkey started up the road. Ruth and Orpah hurried back to their house. They quickly threw their essential belongings into bedsheets, folded them into bundles, and ran after Naomi.

"Wait for us!" Orpah called when she spotted Naomi. Naomi stopped.

"Go back to your mothers' houses," said Naomi when her daughters-in-law caught up. "You have been kind to me and my sons. Now go home."

Ruth said, "We will return with you to your people."

Naomi chortled. "For what? I've no more sons to give you. Listen, daughters, you're young and pretty. Find yourselves husbands while you still can. Come with me, and my bitter life will poison you as sure as a serpent's bite. Turn back, for God is against me."

Orpah kissed Naomi and left.

"God is not against you," said Ruth.

"Save your breath and let me be. Your sister-in-law has

gone back to her people and her gods. Have some sense and do the same."

Ruth tied her bundle to Naomi's donkey. "Wherever you go, I'll go. Wherever you sleep, I'll sleep. Your people are my people. Your God is my God."

Naomi shrugged and continued west toward Israel. Ruth followed.

● ◓ ●

"Look how God has provided for us!" Ruth exclaimed as they drank from a well along the road.

Naomi said nothing.

"For so long I have prayed to see Jerusalem with my own eyes. Now my prayers will be answered."

Naomi took a long, hard look at Ruth and started up the road.

● ◓ ●

The women came to an oasis. Ruth held a date in her hand and said, "Blessed are You, God, Ruler of the Universe, who has created the fruit of the tree."

Naomi did not respond, "Amen."

"The date is one of the seven sacred fruits of Israel," said Ruth. "Does the land truly overflow with their abundance as the Torah says in Deuteronomy chapter eight, verse eight?"

Naomi took a swig from her water bag and said, "Do me a favor. Leave me in peace. All right?"

● ◓ ●

When Naomi and Ruth entered Bethlehem, a crowd met them.

"Naomi?" a woman asked. "Is it really you?"

"Naomi is no more," said Naomi. "God took Naomi as surely as God took her husband and two sons. My name is Bitter."

"Surely God compensates measure for measure," the woman said.

"Yes, God is just," offered another.

The crowd nodded and waited for Naomi to tell them how she had merited God's wrath. Naomi was silent.

"Who is she?" the first woman asked, looking at Ruth.

"She is my daughter-in-law, a Moabite."

"A Moabite," the women murmured, nodding their heads in understanding. Here was the transgression. When Elimelech and Naomi left Bethlehem so long ago, they should have settled in other Israelite lands. It was permissible for children from one Israelite tribe to marry into another. Instead, Elimelech and Naomi had brought their sons to Moab—the land of hedonism and idolatry. There they married idolaters. Clearly, God took note.

"Did she think that God would not exact retribution?" one woman said to her neighbor.

"Yes, God is just," the neighbor replied.

"Let's go," Naomi said to Ruth. "This homecoming is tiring."

Naomi took Ruth to her old house. That afternoon Naomi's oldest friend came to visit.

"Do you believe that I sinned?" Naomi asked.

"It is not for me to judge," her friend replied. "Yet, it is written that God rewards the righteous and punishes transgressors. I think you should look deep inside yourself, pray for forgiveness, and …" the friend added in a whisper with her eyes on Ruth, "send the Moabite away."

Ruth was in the back of the room preparing tea. Naomi looked at her daughter-in-law. Was her friend right? Had God punished her because her sons married Moabites?

Ruth felt Naomi's eyes on her and smiled at her mother-in-law.

It can't be, thought Naomi. Ruth was kind and faithful. She had never tempted Mahlon to become a Moabite. Rather, Ruth followed the laws of Torah and took the God of Israel as her own.

Naomi raised her voice in amplitude as a counterbalance to her friend's whisper. "I do not pretend to understand the ways of God, but I do know that only a child believes that both the good and the bad receive what they deserve. If you but open your eyes, you will see the truth of my words. As for Ruth, do not talk to me about her. She is truer to Torah than any of us."

Naomi's friend excused herself and left the house. Ruth jumped up from tending the hot water and threw her arms around her mother-in-law.

"You are too kind, Mother," she said.

Naomi's arms remained at her sides. "Is the tea ready?"

* * *

"Mother," said Ruth. "The barley harvest is beginning, and our food stocks are low. With your permission, I will glean in the barley fields. After all, the Torah instructs farmers to leave their gleanings for widows."

"Does the Torah explain why God created a world where mothers outlive their children?"

Ruth was silent.

"Go and glean. Maybe God will take note of your kindness to me and learn something about compassion."

Ruth came upon a field and gleaned behind the reapers. The elderly owner of the field, a man named Boaz, noticed Ruth as she cut barley stalks.

"Whose girl is that?" Boaz asked his foreman.

"That, my lord, is the Moabite who came back with Naomi. I have to admit, she is a hard worker—for a Moabite. Some of the men have been talking about having a time with her after work."

Boaz removed the sickle from his belt and pointed it at the foreman. "They are to leave the girl alone," he said.

Boaz dismissed the foreman and went to Ruth.

"Shalom," he said as Ruth stacked her sheaves. Ruth looked up, answered "Shalom," and returned to her work.

"You are finding enough sheaves?" Boaz asked.

Ruth stopped to take a good look at the man—the first person in Bethlehem to offer a kind word. There was a certain familiarity in his looks, Ruth thought. Had Mahlon lived to be a grandfather, he might have resembled this man.

"Yes, I am," she said. "Thank you for your kind words."

"I am Boaz. You are gleaning in my field."

Ruth brushed the sweat and hair from her face.

"Oh, I am sorry. I did not realize ..."

Boaz held up his hand and laughed.

"No need to apologize. It gives me happiness to see you here. I hope my reapers have not bothered you."

"No, they have not bothered me."

"Good. By the threshing floor are water gourds. When you are thirsty, please go and drink."

Ruth bowed her head. "Why has my lord singled me out when I am a foreigner?"

"I have heard all that you have done for your mother-in-law and how you have become a true daughter of Israel."

Ruth lifted her head. Her face was red.

Boaz pointed to Ruth's sheaves. "I see that you have been working hard; it is time for a break. Please share some roasted grain with me."

After eating her fill, Ruth returned to glean. Without her knowledge, Boaz instructed his reapers to pull stalks from their piles for Ruth. That afternoon she collected enough stalks to fill an entire bushel with grain. Ruth came home and put the bushel on the floor next to Naomi. Naomi looked at the overflowing basket of grain. Her eyes grew wide.

"And with whom did you sleep?" she asked.

"What?"

"A full bushel from a single day of gleaning? I think not."

"God forbid! The Torah forbids such relations. I gleaned and beat out the grain myself."

"I see," said Naomi, raising an eyebrow. She ran her hand through the barley. "And where did you glean?"

"In a field owned by a kindly old man named Boaz."

"Boaz!" yelled Naomi. The smiling woman took her startled daughter-in-law into her arms.

For the first time in months, Naomi felt alive, for Boaz was not just any name. Boaz was a well-to-do farmer who must have instructed that stalks be set aside for Ruth; clearly he was attracted to her. And Boaz was even more. He was a redeemer, and this brought life back to Naomi.

She explained to Ruth that Boaz was an uncle of Mahlon, Ruth's dead husband. According to Israelite law, Boaz could marry Ruth, and the children would count as Mahlon's, giving Naomi grandchildren to support her in her old age.

Naomi put her hands together. "Blessed be God who has not failed in kindness and brought you to Boaz."

"Blessed be God's glorious name," added Ruth, who had not heard Naomi utter a blessing in many months.

"Boaz," said Naomi, "can redeem us."

"Boaz will marry me, so I may have children to carry on Mahlon's name?"

"*If* he marries you," answered Naomi, "then your children

count as Mahlon's. But Boaz is under no obligation. It is up to him. Listen, Ruth, do not go to any other fields during the grain harvest."

"Boaz has already instructed me so."

"Wonderful!" Naomi hugged Ruth close. "Now listen closely. Stay near the women and avoid the men in the fields."

"I will, Mother."

Tears ran down Naomi's face. "Since the moment Mahlon brought you home, you have been a virtuous daughter. I know I've been difficult these past months. Can you forgive me?"

"Oh, Mother!" Ruth cried, her face wet as well. "How could I ever be upset with the one who taught me the beauty of Torah? Life has been hard for both of us. I pray now that our troubles are over."

"Amen," said Naomi.

● ▬ ●

The weeks passed and the harvest ended. Ruth came home following her last day of gleaning. When she walked through the door, Naomi asked the same question she asked every day.

"Did Boaz say anything today?"

"No," said Ruth.

"Then it is time to act," said Naomi.

"What do you mean?"

"Ruth, the harvest is over. There is no more reason to go to his fields. He missed his chance to ask you to marry him. So now you have to bring the subject up."

"But, Mother," said Ruth, "you yourself taught me that a daughter of Israel is modest and does not take the initiative with men."

"In normal situations, yes. But this one isn't. Boaz has had enough time. Maybe he hasn't asked you because he fears rejection. After all, he's old enough to be your father."

"I know."

"While a daughter of Israel must be modest, there is one last Torah lesson I must teach you. It may be the most important. It's this: The true genius of our religion is that we don't need to accept the world as it is. We see what the world can become and act to make that happen. God brought the two of you together in order for Boaz to redeem us. But unless *you* act, it won't happen. And if you don't act now, when will you?"

"What would you have me do?"

"Tonight Boaz will be winnowing grain. There will be a harvest party afterward. When the party ends, watch where Boaz sleeps. Then anoint yourself and uncover his feet."

"Naomi, I cannot!"

"By the law of the redeemer it is permissible."

Ruth turned from Naomi and looked out the window.

"Ruth, our lives are in your hands."

Ruth slowly walked to the shelf above her bed and unpacked her oils and perfumes.

⚬ ⬭ ⚬

During the party, Ruth waited in the shadows. After many hours, the revelers stumbled home, and Ruth made her way to Boaz. She found him sleeping next to the grain.

My God, she thought. This is crazy. I can't do this.

Ruth turned to leave, but how could she face Naomi?

"Oh, Mahlon," she whispered into the night air. "I don't know what to do."

An owl hooted in the distance, crickets chirped underfoot, the darkened heavens were silent.

"God is just," said Ruth. "It is God's will that I marry Boaz, so I must."

Ruth took a deep breath, quietly pulled back Boaz's blanket, and lay down by his side, her body rigid. Boaz's gentle breathing relaxed Ruth, and soon her body began to crave the warmth that a man provided. She curled closer to Boaz and slowly put her hand on his chest.

Boaz gave a start and woke up to find a woman in his bed. "Who are you?" he asked.

"It is I, Ruth, your handmaid. Spread your robe over me, for you are a redeeming kinsman."

Boaz turned to Ruth and kissed her.

"May God bless you, Ruth. You are a true daughter of Israel. You, who could have turned to a younger man, have chosen to perpetuate your late husband's good name. I will do as you ask. Stay the night. Tomorrow I will set things right."

● ◌ ●

Ruth rose before dawn and returned home. Naomi greeted her with a cup of hot tea.

"You did well, daughter. Now Boaz will settle the matter."

Boaz, however, had not avoided asking for Ruth's hand for fear of rejection. Rather, he knew that Mahlon had a closer relative named Plony on whom the duty to redeem fell. Plony needed to waive his obligation before Boaz could act.

Boaz went to the city gates where the elders of Bethlehem gathered. Boaz saw Plony and called him over.

"Your kinswoman Naomi must sell her land. Since you are the closest redeemer, you have first right to the land. If you decide not to redeem it, I will redeem it."

Plony replied, "I will redeem it."

Boaz continued, "You realize that when you acquire Naomi's property, you also acquire Ruth the Moabite, the widow of Mahlon, in order to perpetuate his estate."

"If I buy Naomi's estate, it will go to the child of a Moabite?"

The elders nodded.

"I waive my right of redemption," said Plony. "The Moabite is yours."

* * *

Boaz and Ruth married a month later. Eight months passed and Ruth bore a son, Obed.

By the time Obed was born, the women of Bethlehem had changed their opinions of Ruth. They now saw Ruth as a God-fearing daughter of Israel.

"Since arriving back in Bethlehem, Naomi has converted Ruth from idolatry to the ways of God," said one.

"You would think Naomi would be grateful when we pointed out that her bad luck was due to Ruth's idolatry," said another.

"She won't ever thank us."

Later, the women said to Naomi, "Blessed be the Lord who through your daughter-in-law brought you a son to sustain you in your old age. Ruth loves you better than seven sons."

Naomi took the child and held him to her heart.

"I have waited lifetimes for you. I thought that you would never arrive."

Naomi wiped a tear from her eye.

"You have given meaning to my suffering."

Naomi looked into Obed's eyes and said, "Every single day and every single night I mourn for my sons whose cups shattered before they were filled. Perhaps their deaths were random. Perhaps they sinned before God. Or perhaps their deaths were part of God's plan. Maybe it was decided in heaven that Ruth and Boaz needed to marry. I don't know. Obed, I don't understand God, but I am grateful for your life. May you grow and bring honor to your family and your people."

And he did. Obed lived an honorable life, his son Jesse lived an honorable life, and Jesse's son, Obed's grandson, David, became Israel's greatest king.

The Suicide
Bomber

imes were good in Israel. War was a dim memory of the past. Fatted lambs grazed contentedly next to vineyards bursting with pregnant grapes. The people were complacent, and they therefore forgot about God.

"It's only when they're in trouble that they remember You and offer up sacrifices," Gabriella groused to God.

God sighed, "I can barely remember what roasted lamb smells like."

Besides forgetting God, the Israelites neglected to pay attention to their Philistine neighbors stockpiling spears, arrows, and javelins. Instead of banding together to fight the menace, the Israelites lived in blissful ignorance until one day the Philistines marched in and forced them to pay tribute.

The Israelites quickly sacrificed their best lambs and cried for God's help.

"Let 'em help themselves," Gabriella counseled.

Though God did savor the delicious aroma of lamb, God decided that the Israelites did not yet deserve deliverance. For forty years Israel lived under the thumb of the Philistines.

● ◼ ●

One day God came upon Gabriella and announced, "It's time."

"And not a moment too soon," said the angel, stretching out her back. For what seemed like eons, Gabriella had been colliding atomic particles at light speeds in order to create some new elements for God. Her arms ached from throwing the particles over and over again, her eyes were bloodshot, and her wings were stiff as rock. "I sure could use a vacation."

"Vacation?" God looked at the chief angel quizzically. "Who said vacation? No. It's time to save the Israelites. We need to find them a leader."

Gabriella's halo drooped.

"What about that guy, Ody, from the Judah tribe? I thought we agreed about him? You know the guy with the plan to sneak a giant wooden camel into the Philistine capital and ..."

God put up a hand. "They called him a 'quill-necked know-it-all.'"

"Hmm," mused Gabriella. "I guess brainy guys make them feel insecure. And that was after the debacle with that woman—what was her name—Lisa Strada or something. Good thing I was there to save her neck from the mob."

God nodded. "They weren't ready for a female leader. Too bad. Getting all the women on both the Israelite and Philistine sides to stop having sex with the men until everyone agreed to turn their swords into plowshares could have worked."

"Yep," said Gabriella. "The only force more powerful than their thirst for blood is their thirst for sex." The angel stretched out her wings. "So what's the plan, Boss?"

"Time to give the people the leader they want."

"Your double-dose-of-brawn-hold-the-brains type?"

"Yep," God said. "Standard issue. People always wind up with the leaders they deserve."

God turned to go.

"Boss?"

God looked back.

"Boss, you like these people. How come?"

God smiled. "With them, I'm never bored."

For many years, Manoah and his wife could not conceive a child, so Manoah's wife prayed to God.

"Blessed are You, God, Ruler of the Universe, Creator of All, the One who understands the misery of a poor, childless woman. Send me but one son, and I will dedicate his life to You."

The prayer was perfectly timed to God's latest plan, so Gabriella went down to work out the terms of birth.

Manoah's wife stood mouth agape as the angel jumped out of a particularly large cumulous cloud, floated down an air current, and landed next to the woman.

Gabriella folded in her wings, unfurled a parchment, and removed a quill from her robes. She licked the end of the quill and said, "We heard your prayer and are seriously considering your proposal." The angel scratched a few words onto the parchment and continued. "So. If We grant you a son, you will really dedicate him to God? Be honest."

"You have my word," insisted Manoah's wife.

"The word of a human is as permanent as the daily wind, strong in the morning, but by dusk, gone." Gabriella searched the terrified woman's eyes and said, "Nevertheless, you will have a son."

"Oh, thank you, thank you, thank you," she said.

"By dedicating his life to God, your son will be expected to save Israel from the hand of the Philistines. Therefore, there are two conditions we must insist upon," Gabriella said to Manoah's wife.

"Yes, yes, of course. Anything, anything."

"While you are pregnant you may drink neither wine nor anything alcoholic."

"I won't, I promise, I won't."

"This prohibition also binds your son. No wine, no grape juice, nor even a single grape may ever cross his lips."

"Be assured that he will never even touch a grape. I will have my husband immediately uproot our vineyard."

"Condition two: Your son's hair must never be cut. He's to be a Nazir to God and must not concern himself with his looks. Agreed?"

"Of course," Manoah's wife agreed. "I will do everything you ask. Just let me have a son."

"Your prayer is to be granted," said Gabriella, "but like most prayers granted, the sorrows brought with it may equal or outweigh the joys."

Gabriella departed, and Manoah's wife told her husband all that had happened. He didn't believe her, so Gabriella had to return and repeat herself. Upon seeing the angel with his own eyes, Manoah quickly prepared a sacrificial goat. He heard Gabriella mutter, "Men," just prior to her ascending to heaven with the smoke of the goat.

⚫ ⬬ ⚫

Nine months after Gabriella's visit, Samson was born. As soon as he was able to grab a baby rattle, Manoah could not pry it from his hand. When a group of four-year-olds decided to build a fort with sticks and small rocks, Samson brought a boulder to be the castle. No one in the village had ever seen a child or adult with such strength.

To help Samson fulfill his destiny of freeing the Israelites from the hated Philistines, Manoah tried to teach him martial arts. But there wasn't anything about warfare that a shepherd could teach a six-year-old boy who could scare wolves by glaring at them. Manoah, however, was able to give Samson one lesson that always stuck with him: Always pay your enemy back with interest.

As a boy, Samson needed to use this lesson only once. When he was eight years old, the fifteen-year-old village bully came upon Samson loading flour bags onto the family cart.

"Let me help you," the bully snickered, tripping Samson.

Samson got up, brushed the dirt off, and shook his head. As Samson felt his long locks of hair slap against his body, the spirit of God came upon him.

The bully's "ha-ha-ha," quickly became "whoa, whoa, whoa," as Samson lifted him high above his head and threw him into the cart, breaking the leg he had tripped Samson with.

As a young man, Samson was friendless for two reasons. His gigantic stature inspired fear into the other young men of the village, and his parents had vowed to keep Samson away from alcohol and other youthful vices. So while the other young men went to parties, got drunk, and fooled around with girls, Samson studied the laws of the Nazirite.

As part of his Nazirite training, Samson was sent alone to the mountains to build up his spirit and learn the will of God. It was common Israelite knowledge that the mountains were the best place to hear the voice of God. Moses had taught that outside the hustle and bustle of the village, the severed connection between human and Divine could be restored.

Yet, even in the mountains, the voice of God eluded Samson. The only sounds he heard on his retreats were the birds singing, the wind whistling, and his own heart beating. Still, Samson loved the mountains. There was nothing better than sitting amid the seas of wildflowers blanketing the mountainsides. It was here that Samson came to love beauty. Before returning to his village, he would always scour the mountains to find the prettiest flowers to bring home.

● ⬭ ●

Samson reached adulthood, and Manoah decided to find a wife for his son.

"Son, it's time for you to marry. I reached an agreement with my trading partner from the tribe of Gad. He will give you the hand of his daughter Dori. Mazel Tov."

"Is she beautiful?" Samson asked.

"My son, beauty fades. She is a God-fearing girl who can keep a good home. She will make a fitting wife for you."

"She's ugly?"

"I think she's attractive."

But when Samson met her, he was not satisfied. Just as he picked only the prettiest flowers, Samson wanted the prettiest girl for his wife. Manoah brought another girl, then another, then another. Samson rejected each one.

"I give up!" Manoah said after Samson rejected the tenth girl. "I don't know any other men with daughters. Find your own wife."

Samson arose and walked the length of Israel searching for the one beauty to make his wife. He knew she existed somewhere, but after searching all twelve Israelite tribes, he came up empty.

While bemoaning his bad luck, Samson was in the market in Timnath when he saw her—the most beautiful, exotic, black-haired beauty he had ever laid eyes on. The fact that she was a Philistine girl did nothing to subdue his desire. Samson didn't care where she was from; all he knew was that he wanted her. He stared at her as she plucked grapes from a cluster and placed them one after another in her mouth. Samson felt a warm, tingling sensation under his loincloth and knew that she was the one.

"I've seen a Philistine girl from Timnath that I want you to get me for my wife," Samson told his parents.

"In all of Israel you can't find a girl?" asked his mother.

"A Philistine?" said his father. "Are you trying to kill me?"

Samson's mind was made up. There was nothing his parents could do to convince him otherwise, so they journeyed to Timnath to make the arrangements. Along the way, they passed a vineyard. Samson wanted to bring his love a gift of grapes. Despite his mother's pleas, he stepped into the vineyard where he met a young lion twitching his tail. Samson shook his locks and felt the spirit of God flow through him. He caught the lion in the middle of its pounce, grabbed its mane and yanked, breaking its neck.

"My mane gives me life, yours brought you death," Samson said to the dead beast, and then he continued with his parents to Timnath.

When Samson strode into Timnath, the people hid from the man-giant.

"My son desires to marry one of your girls," Manoah called out as they walked the deserted streets.

The shocked chief came out, spoke to Manoah, found the girl's father, and called a meeting of the Philistine elders. The elders debated. On one hand, how could they not be happy that the strongest Israelite was marrying one of their daughters, thereby ensuring that the Israelites would not launch a rebellion against their rule? On the other hand, no one fully trusted this muscle-bound Nazirite with the crazy hair. Was this a scheme to start a revolt? In the end, the elders agreed to the marriage, and the girl's father told Manoah that the girl would need some time to ready herself.

Samson and his parents returned home. On the way back, Samson again stopped at the vineyard. He found the dead lion's body filled with honey and bees. He stuck in his hand and took some honey.

"Nice allegorical touch," God congratulated Gabriella. "Sweet honey from a nonkosher animal." God paused in thought. "I just hope this one can survive the Philistines' sting."

● ━ ●

At Samson's wedding the tongues of the Philistines loosened as the wine flowed down their gullets. All latent fears of the Israelite strongman were forgotten.

"Shower us with your Hebrew wisdom," one young man laughed. "You're one of the People of the Book."

The teetotaling Samson uncurled his arm from the waist of his wife and curled his arm into a huge muscle.

"This is my book," he said. "But you want Hebrew wisdom. All right, here's a riddle. I'll bet you thirty linen sheets and thirty suits of clothing that you can't guess it within the seven days of the wedding feast."

"We would hate to steal the wealth of the new groom," one lionhearted man said, "but if you insist, bring it on."

"All right," Samson said. "Here it is. From the eater came out food, and out of the strong came sweetness."

Samson grinned as the Philistine foreheads furrowed and their smiles disappeared.

After three days the now-sober young men realized that they needed to act, or they would be out lots of shekels. They sent a messenger to Samson's wife.

"Find out the answer to your husband's riddle, or else we'll burn you and your father's house."

The frightened bride had no choice. That night she traced

the outline of Samson's chest with her finger and said, "I have a favor to ask, my love."

"Anything, ask me anything and it's yours."

"Tell me the answer to the riddle."

"Don't ask that."

"But a husband tells a wife everything. You must hate me."

"I haven't even told my parents," Samson said, and he rolled over to sleep.

The next night Samson's wife came into the bedroom and asked again. Again Samson refused to tell her.

"Then tonight I will sleep in my sister's room."

The next night, Samson's wife came into the bedroom, climbed into bed, and stroked Samson's long locks.

"Please," she whispered.

Samson grit his teeth, hissed, "Never!" and turned away.

The next night Samson's wife stood in the bedroom door wearing a tight-fitting bodice that hugged her hourglass figure.

"Tell me and you may do what you wish to me all night long."

Samson's urges finally overtook his Nazirite training.

"All right, all right!" he bellowed. "Stop tormenting me!"

Samson told her the answer and she upheld her side of the bargain.

*   *   *

"What is sweeter than honey, and what is stronger than a lion," the smiling young men said to Samson.

Samson narrowed his eyes at the smug men.

"If you hadn't plowed with my heifer, you wouldn't have known."

"All's fair in love and war," one man ventured.

"No truer words have ever left your mouth," replied Samson. "You'll get your linens and clothing by sunset."

"Take your time," said the same man. "We're in no rush."

"I am," said Samson, heading down the road and shaking his head violently to bring on the spirit of God. He killed the first thirty Philistines he met and took their clothes. He gave them to the men he owed and returned to his father's house.

Shocked at Samson's behavior and under the impression that his son-in-law had abandoned his daughter, Samson's father-in-law gave his daughter to one of Samson's companions. A short while later, Samson returned to Timnath to claim his wife.

"I thought you hated her, so I gave her to another. But," he quickly added upon seeing a dangerous look on Samson's face, "I have a younger daughter you can take. She's prettier and, of course, a virgin."

Samson, however, was not interested in making peace with any of the dishonorable Philistines; rather, he wanted war.

"What you did to me, I'll pay back and be blameless."

Instead of taking his wife's sister, Samson took three hundred foxes. He separated the foxes into pairs and tied the tails of each pair together. Where their tails met, he stuck a burning torch and let all one hundred and fifty pairs loose in the Philistine fields, destroying the standing grain, the vineyards, and the olive trees.

The shocked Philistines watched their food supply go up in flames and said to each other, "Who do we blame for this?"

Though the answer, of course, was that crazy Israelite muscleman, laying blame on him was dangerous. So they burned Samson's wife and father-in-law instead.

Upon hearing what they had done to his wife, Samson angrily slaughtered every Philistine soldier he could find.

"This guy makes Achilles look like Mahatma Gandhi," Gabriella remarked to God.

God sighed. "I know. I should have added the tagline to the Sixth Commandment, 'for violence always leads to more violence.' "

The Philistine generals surveyed the damage done and surrounded Judah, the largest Israelite tribe, with their forces.

"What do you want with us?" the nervous men asked. "Don't we already give you half of our crops every year?"

The Philistine general replied, "Either bring us Samson, so we can do to him as he did to us, or we'll slaughter you."

Three thousand men of Judah found Samson and said, "What are you doing to us? They're going to wipe us out because of you!"

Samson arose. "I paid them back for what they did to me."

"And then some," a Judah elder replied. The three thousand men pressed closely around Samson. "We're here to bind you and hand you over to them. Better to sacrifice one than have the whole nation destroyed."

Samson put out his hands for the Judah men to bind with two new ropes. They brought him to the Philistines.

"Hah! You brainless son of a whore!" the Philistines shouted as they brought out their knives to slash Samson. "Now we've got you!"

Samson shook his head and the spirit of God flowed through him; he broke through the thick ropes as if they were two strands of hair.

"All right!" Samson shouted. "Let's see who's got who." He picked up the jawbone of a donkey that was lying by his feet.

The terrified Philistines closest to Samson screamed and tripped over each other trying to escape. Using the jaw as a truncheon, Samson sped through the Philistines, massacring them as if he were killing ants. Within a few hours, one thousand dead Philistines littered the landscape.

Samson surveyed his handiwork with a grim smile, tossed the jawbone aside, and fell to his knees, exhausted.

"God," he said, lifting his head to the sky, "you gave me the power against the Philistines; now I'm about to die of thirst. If I go to a Philistine well, I'll fall into the hands of these uncircumcised heathens. God, I pray to you. Give me water."

"Hallelujah!" Gabriella mocked. "After all these years, Samson has finally found God. Nothing like the Angel of Death fixing her eye sockets on a guy to get him to put his hands together."

Samson continued. "I promise to stay away from Philistine women from now on. All right?"

Gabriella guffawed. "Why do they vow things they can't deliver? Listen, God, all this carnage is making me lose my appetite. Let me save the guy and call it a day."

God nodded and Gabriella sent a stream of water from an empty tooth socket of the jawbone. Samson was saved.

As for the Philistines, they were in full retreat. For the next twenty years, the Israelites did not pay tribute to them.

* * *

Like a good Nazirite, Samson never cut his hair and he avoided grape products. It would, however, be a long stretch to say that he dedicated his life to God. Rather, Samson dedicated his life to satisfying his libido. He loved women and needed to have one every night, and sometimes during the day as well.

Samson explained to his father, "Some men need to read from the sacred book every day. Some men need to eat fine food every day. Some men need to exercise every day. Me, I need a beautiful girl every day or else I don't feel right."

As undisputed military leader of Israel, Samson had a vast number of women to choose from. And even when he wasn't in the mood for a romp, women might find their buttocks or breasts squeezed by the warlord.

The men of Israel were dismayed that their wives and daughters were fair game, but there was nothing they could do. Without Samson, the Philistines would be back, so they overlooked his philandering and tried to hide their women as best they could.

As for Samson's vow about Philistine women, it lasted almost half a year—until a beautiful Philistine prostitute in Gaza caught his eye. Samson began visiting her a few times each year.

One night when Samson was in Gaza, a group of Philistine warriors hid by the city gates to ambush him at first light. The prostitute warned Samson, so he arose at midnight to find fifty armed men sleeping at the locked gate. Samson grinned, shook his hair, and lifted the entire gate, along with its two posts anchored into the ground, onto his shoulders. He set the gates on top of a mountain overlooking the city, and the Philistines saw that they were not about to regain control over the Israelites that day.

● ⬤ ●

After almost twenty years of keeping Israel safe, Samson fell in love. Once again the object of his love was a Philistine. Her name was Delilah. She was the only woman who could fully satisfy Samson, so he moved in with her.

The Philistine lords, desperate to once again rule Israel, approached Delilah and said, "Find out where his great strength lies, so we can rid our people of this menace."

"But I love him," she replied.

"Each of us will pay you eleven hundred pieces of silver."

Delilah counted the lords and did the math. She could be rich. And what was love? How long would Samson be enamored of her before seeking out a new beauty?

"Okay," she said.

That night as they prepared for bed, Delilah said to Samson, "Tell me where your strength comes from so you can be tied up and tortured."

Samson loved Delilah's bed games and said, "All right, tie me up with seven moist drawstrings."

So she did it.

Once he was tied tight, Delilah shouted, "The Philistines are coming for you!"

Samson shook his head, broke the drawstrings, and made love to Delilah, while the hiding Philistines crept away.

The next night Delilah said, "You lied to me last night, Samson. Now really tell me where your power is."

"All right. This time use new ropes; that will overpower me."

So she did.

Delilah tied the ropes even tighter than the night before and then shouted, "The Philistines are coming for you!"

Samson shook his head, tore through the ropes, and again the chagrined Philistines crept away.

The next night Delilah said, "You are mocking me, Samson. Now tell me, really, how I can tie you up."

"All right. Take the seven locks of my hair and tie them to the wooden roller." Samson pointed to the wooden roller on Delilah's loom.

So she did.

Once she was satisfied that Samson could not move his head, Delilah shouted, "The Philistines are coming for you!"

Samson shook his head, busted the loom, and once again the story repeated itself.

The next night Delilah said, "Samson, until you tell me, truthfully, where your strength comes from, I'm not sleeping with you. I'm serious, no games."

Samson, worn out from the previous nights' escapades, rolled over and went to sleep.

The next night Delilah said the same thing. Samson told her to tie him with bronze chains. Delilah didn't believe him and walked out of the room.

The next night Delilah came to the door and said, "Tell me the truth or you can just play with yourself."

"All right, already, all right," said Samson, more than ready to dispense with abstinence. "It's my hair. If someone cuts my hair, I'll lose my strength. Satisfied? Now get into bed."

Delilah smiled and climbed in. After a long night, the exhausted Samson laid his head on Delilah's knees and fell asleep. While he slept, a Philistine barber came and cut off his hair.

The truth of the matter was that Samson's strength came from the muscles that God had endowed him with. Unfortunately for Samson, he believed his mother's story that his strength came from his hair.

When Delilah shouted that the Philistines were coming, Samson woke up and shook his head. Upon realizing that his hair was gone, his self-confidence, the spirit of God, vanished. The mighty Samson, protector of Israel, slayer of Philistines, became as helpless as a newborn baby.

The Philistines grabbed Samson, but Delilah stopped them from killing him.

"Do with him as you like, but let him live," she said.

So the Philistines gouged out his eyes and threw their hated enemy into a dungeon.

● ● ●

The weakened Samson sat alone in the dark cell.

"I lusted after my eyes. Now that I'm blind I can finally see clearly. Maybe it's not too late to serve God."

As hair slowly sprouted from his bald head, Samson felt his confidence and strength return. A few months passed and three thousand Philistine men, women, and princes gathered at the Temple of Dagon to offer sacrifices to their god for delivering Samson to them.

It was a great celebration, with the Philistines singing, dancing, and drinking well into the night. When the celebrants were significantly drunk, they started chanting, "We want Samson! We want Samson!"

A half-dozen men stumbled down to Samson's cell and shouted, "Showtime, musclehead!" One man lassoed a rope around Samson's waist, while the others stood ready with stout sticks. Samson let himself be dragged off to the temple.

Standing outside the temple, Samson heard the crowd inside scream his name. A young boy was ordered to take Samson by the hand and lead him into the temple.

"Look!" someone heckled. "A child has tamed the big, bad Samson!"

The crowd erupted in laughter.

"These uncircumcised heathens think they can toy with me," Samson said to himself. "But I'm not done yet. My life for the honor of my people, for the glory of God. I'll give them a terror that they will not soon forget."

"Boy," he said to his handler. "Grant me one request as I shall soon be dead. My throat is parched. Bring me water from the well. While you are gone, put me between the pillars that hold up the temple, so I can lean against them."

The boy, terrified both from having his hand enveloped in Samson's humongous hand, as well as being surrounded by a lynch mob of three thousand, quickly ran outside.

The mocking laughter grew.

"How about a glass of wine, you stupid Israelite Nazirite!"

A hailstorm of rotten, fermented grapes struck Samson. Rather than flinch, a wicked smile formed on his face.

"My Lord, God," Samson prayed, "remember and strengthen me this one time, so I can take revenge on the Philistines for one of my two eyes."

Samson shook his head and his hair energized him. He grasped both pillars and first leaned into the left one and then the right one.

As the pillars began to move from their foundations, Samson said, "For your glory, God, I end my life to kill Philistines."

The Philistines quickly sobered and screamed, "The crazy bastard is trying to kill us all! Help!"

But there was no help for the Philistines. Samson pushed the left pillar over and screamed, "Adonai is God!" as the roof tumbled down, killing all three thousand Philistines. Samson killed more Philistines during his suicide than the total he had killed in all the years he fought them.

● ● ●

"Well?" asked Gabriella.

"Well, what?" God replied.

"What do You think about him killing the innocent with the guilty and himself as well?"

"Sometimes when humans reach great heights and acknowledge Me as the source of their inspiration, My heart swells with great love. On the other hand, there is nothing sadder than to be named as the motivation for carnage like this. This is not My hope for the world."

Samson's family came, found his body amid the temple wreckage, and buried Samson between Zorah and Eshtaol. Altogether Samson had protected Israel for twenty years.

The Second Sling

The morning lark sang, and David, a young shepherd, lifted his head from the lambskin he used as his pillow. To his left, the full moon was dipping over the western hills. To his right, the sky was aflame from the fiery oranges and reds of the sunrise.

David sat up to take a deep breath of the crisp air. The lark sang again.

He stood and addressed the bird, "Oh, how I wish I had the purity of heart to sing my praise as beautifully and sincerely as you."

David picked up his lyre, strummed a chord, and sang:

> *The heavens announce the glory of God,*
> *The sky tells of God's handiwork.*
> *The Earth is Adonai's and all that it holds.*
> *God renews my life and guides me along the right path.*
> *Hallelujah, Adonai, Hallelujah.*

David watched the golden sun rise over the horizon, put his lyre down, and nudged his sleeping friend with his toe.

"Elhanon," he said. "Wake up."

"Go 'way," Elhanon replied and wrapped his blanket tighter around his shoulders.

For a moment David stood bemused; then he cupped his hands around his mouth and yelled, "Lion!"

Like a surprised antelope, Elhanon leapt out of his blanket. In one motion he took his sling, loaded it with a stone, twirled it around his head, and shouted, "Where is it?"

"Good morning, friend," David said. "Beautiful day, isn't it?"

Elhanon stared at David in disgust and flung the rock at a tamarisk tree thirty cubits away. The smack of the rock hitting the tree dead center made the nearby sheep jump.

"Nice shot," said David.

"Next time you wake me with a lion tale, you'll find a rock right here." Elhanon pointed to his forehead.

David blew on the embers from the night before and started a fire. He placed a pot of water on and picked up his lyre.

"Friend," Elhanon continued, "the instrument you need practice with isn't that stringed thing. What are you going to do when a lion really comes and I'm not around? Sing to it? *Oh, sweet lion, please, oh please, return my little lamb.* You need to learn how to use that."

Elhanon pointed at David's pristine-looking sling.

"What do you mean? I once saved a lamb from a lion."

"Luck, my friend. Smacking a lion with your staff might have been brave, but really, really stupid."

David offered Elhanon leftover flat bread and goat jerky. They ate and drank tea.

After finishing, Elhanon took up his sling and, sounding like a teacher delivering a lesson, said, "Your sling is your best friend. It can defend you against enemies both beast and man."

"God protects me," David said.

"Well, God never said no to any extra help. Here. Look. The first thing you have to do is find the right rock. Half the size of your fist and smooth. Those are the best."

Elhanon picked up a rock and held it in front of David's face before slipping it into his sling.

"Technique is everything," Elhanon said. "Watch."

David looked. But instead of watching Elhanon twirl the sling, David stared at his friend's rippling muscles and earnest face.

"So much beauty God has filled the world with," he said to himself.

Elhanon released the stone and hit the tree again. The sound woke David from his thoughts.

"Okay," said Elhanon, "you try."

David picked up the first rock he found, dropped it into his sling, twirled it a few times around his head, and flung it. The stone landed ten cubits behind him.

"Premature ejaculation," Elhanon grinned. "You know about that, eh? You're releasing way too early. Keep practicing. You'll get it." Elhanon gathered his blanket and some food. "I'm going to check on the pastures north of the hills. If they're good, I think we should move the sheep."

David watched Elhanon walk away and wondered why he looked at boys in the same way he looked at girls.

●　◼　●

"I don't think Saul's working out," God commented to Gabriella.

"None of your leaders ever do," replied the angel.

"Moses was good," God said.

"Moses, Moses, Moses. That's the only guy you ever bring up. You were so hot for Saul. What was that you said? *He even looks like a king, so tall, so handsome … so mental.* The guy is seriously schizophrenic."

"I've decided on a new guy. The young shepherd David."

"David?"

"His psalms are terrific."

"He's a boy, and he's not exactly macho."

"A vastly overrated leadership quality. Go down and tell my prophet Samuel."

● ━ ●

If Samuel were to have been born three thousand years later in the twentieth century, he would have stood on a street corner in a major metropolis preaching the word of God. The police would have known him by name, and some passersby would have smiled indulgently at the man with the matted hair, ragged clothing, and piercing blue eyes who was in need of a shower and a shave. Most people, however, would have simply ignored the ranting man. But in 1000 B.C.E., Samuel was not a man to either humor or ignore. He was the mouthpiece of God, whose words made kings quake.

Samuel was at the house of Jesse the Bethlehemite with instructions to anoint one of Jesse's sons as king to replace Saul.

Eliav, Jesse's firstborn, came before Samuel. He was a tall and handsome man. Very kinglike, thought Samuel, as he undid his horn of anointing oil.

"He's not the one," God said to Samuel.

"But look at him," replied Samuel. "He's tall and strong, the perfect king."

"So was Saul. You look at his looks. I look into his heart."

"Sorry," Samuel said to Eliav. "Send me your brother."

Jesse's second oldest, Avinadav, came before Samuel.

God said, "No."

Samuel said, "Next," and this was repeated until each of Jesse's seven eldest sons came before him.

Samuel sighed, thinking that being a prophet had to be the world's most exasperating job.

"Are these all of them?" he asked Jesse.

"There's one more. He's out tending sheep."
"Call him in."

∙ ● ●

David bathed and put on his Sabbath robes before greeting Samuel.

"Come on," said Jesse. "Samuel's been waiting long enough."

"I'm almost ready." David looked in the mirror, readjusted his robe, and combed his hair.

"Going to a wedding?" mocked Eliav.

"I'm ready," David said. He entered Samuel's room where he found the prophet studying the Torah.

Jesse announced, "My last son, David."

Samuel saw a youth with red cheeks and sparkling brown eyes. He waited for God's "No," for not only was this son but a boy, he also seemed to Samuel more pretty than handsome. The prophet could not imagine soldiers taking orders from him.

As Samuel waited for the Divine veto, David asked, "May I play God's prophet a song?"

David turned to Avinadav. "Brother, would you mind fetching my lyre?"

While Avinadav left to do David's bidding, David turned to another brother and said, "I was called so quickly from the flock, I didn't have a chance to tell Elhanon. Could you bring this to him?"

David handed his brother a bundle of goat jerky.

"And here is ointment for the hoof of an injured ewe. Elhanon will show you which one."

Without a word, the brother left with the jerky and ointment. Avinadav brought in David's lyre. David sang:

I will love You, O God.
You are my strength
You are my rock, my protector, my redeemer.
You are the one I trust, the one I call upon in danger.
With You by my side I shall never be afraid.

Samuel's eyes welled up with tears, and God whispered in a choked voice, "Yes."

"Come here, son," Samuel commanded. "God has singled you out to lead the nation of Israel, to be our king."

"Be k-k-king!" David sputtered. "Saul is king. I ... I'm a shepherd boy."

"Nevertheless," Samuel continued, "God has commanded it so. Kneel."

David stood in shock until his father placed his hands on his shoulders and gently pushed David to his knees. While David's brothers watched, Samuel took his horn of olive oil and generously poured it over David's bowed head.

"With the power vested in me by God, I hereby anoint you, David son of Jesse, King of Israel."

As the oil streamed down his hair and head, David clearly heard a voice: "I will be with you in all that you do. Don't be afraid. You will triumph over your enemies and become a great king. But for now, keep it a secret."

Samuel tied the horn back onto his belt and said, "Arise, King David. I am at your service."

David stood. Samuel, Jesse, and all of David's brothers bowed to him. For the past few minutes, David had felt as if he were in a dream. But as he looked at everyone kneeling before him, David realized that he was no longer a simple shepherd boy. His flock was no longer the family sheep, but all of Israel. A new responsibility rested on his shoulders like a full-grown ram; his heart beat so hard, David felt it might burst.

David cried, "Please, Samuel, Father, brothers. Saul is still the anointed one of Israel. When my time arrives, I shall serve as king. Until then, I shall simply be David."

* * *

Though David insisted on simply being David, life rarely conforms to one's desires. The Philistines, Israel's belligerent coastal neighbors, attacked small Israelite villages when King Saul and his army were away.

"We can't let them get away without a fight," David told his brothers. "It's up to us."

"But how, brother king?" Avinadav asked. "The Philistines outnumber us and have better weapons."

David looked to heaven.

Adonai, fight my enemies.
Take up Your shield, spear, and javelin against those who persecute us.

David turned to Avinidav.

Their kings won't be delivered by
large forces of strong soldiers,
For their great power will not help them escape.

"David," said Eliav, "we need more weapons besides your psalms."

"I agree, brother," David replied. "We'll use surprise and trickery to inspire fear in the Philistines' hearts."

So David, his brothers, and their friends attacked the Philistines through hit-and-run ambushes. Though David's training as a soldier consisted of the few slingshot lessons Elhanon had given him, David was the guerrilla band's undisputed leader, because there was none braver, nor a better strategist.

Once when the Philistines were returning from what they thought was a successful raid, David stationed Elhanon at the mouth of a narrow gorge. As the Philistines passed, Elhanon slung three stones, killing one soldier and wounding two others. The furious Philistines chased Elhanon into the gorge. They cornered him where the gorge dead-ended.

"We've got the bastard now!" cried the commander.

But as the commander gripped his spear tighter, Elhanon disappeared behind some rocks, and David signaled his hidden men. The men rose as one and threw their javelins, skewering four soldiers. As the bewildered Philistines stood staring at their fallen comrades, David led a charge and five more Philistines fell before the troop retreated in terror.

David stood amid the dead soldiers and stared at his blood-drenched sword.

"Oh, God," he said, "why can't men be satisfied with the gifts that You bestow on them so freely? Why do men need to take what is not theirs? It would be much more pleasant to sit under a tree and play music to You, instead of this."

Before God could answer, Elhanon took David's sword and wiped it clean.

"If I didn't see it with my own eyes, I'd swear you were a different person," said Elhanon.

"I am," said David, sheathing his sword. "Though I can't say if the change has been for the better. My innocence is a dim memory of the past."

● ◍ ◍

While David's star was rising, King Saul suffered a great depression, because the spirit of God mysteriously left him. Saul stalked through the rooms of his palace and raged at his counselors, his servants, and anyone who came into his sight.

"If it pleases His Majesty," his chief counselor cautiously spoke, after Saul had run his spear through a couch. "Perhaps I may seek out a man to play music that relaxes and brings joy to you."

"Anything," cried Saul. "Anything for a little peace."

"Very good, Sire. I know a son of Jesse the Bethlehemite who is not only an excellent musician, but a brave soldier full of wisdom beyond his years, and handsome as well."

"Bring him," commanded Saul, and a messenger fetched David.

David entered the king's throne room and was struck by the heaps of food, the armed guards, the exceedingly comely women, and a singularly handsome man, Jonathan, Saul's eldest son.

"Play!" commanded Saul, and David snapped back to reality.

David took up his lyre and sang:

> God is my light and salvation.
> Whom shall I fear?

As David played, Saul's breathing lengthened and eased. His hands, which as of late were always tensed around his spear, relaxed. Saul's evil spirit left him.

Jonathan was amazed at his father's transformation and stared at the beautiful young man who had wrought this miracle. Jonathan met and held David's eyes until Saul said, "David, son of Jesse the Bethlehemite, stay as one of my arms-bearers."

"Of course, Your Majesty," David said.

"I will see to his housing," Jonathan offered.

"Very well," agreed Saul.

So David moved into Saul's palace. During the day he played music for the king, while in the evening, he and Jonathan shared the secrets of their hearts and became soulmates.

The Philistines launched a major offensive against Israel. They were determined to conquer the pesky Israelites once and for all. And they brought their new weapon, the giant Goliath of Gat, who was a head taller than a camel. His armor weighed five thousand brass shekels. His spear could not be hefted by two grown men.

The Israelites lined up on one side of the Ela Valley. The Philistines lined up on the other. The Israelites quaked at the sight of Goliath standing in front of the Philistine forces.

"Why should we fight a battle?" thundered the giant. "Choose your champion to fight me. If he wins, we'll be your slaves. If I beat him, you are ours."

The Israelites looked at each other and fell silent. King Saul, Israel's mightiest warrior, hunched over to make himself look small. The Israelites began to edge backward. Some fled.

David looked at the giant with a feeling of disdain mingled with fear. He wanted to spit on the ground and curse the Philistine, but the sight of the monster turned his mouth into a desert. Yet, David felt the spirit of God with him, and he saw that this would be the perfect opportunity to prove himself worthy to be Israel's future king.

David said to the soldiers near him, "Who is this uncircumcised Philistine that he should taunt the army of the living God?"

David's brother Eliav heard David and, fearful that David was going to do something rash, said, "What are you doing here? You should be tending our sheep. Go on. Get out of here."

But David went to King Saul and said, "I will fight him."

"No," said Saul. "You're a boy. Goliath will kill you like a lion ripping apart a lamb."

"Once a lion came to my father's flock and took a lamb. I chased it down and killed it with my staff. And this uncircumcised Philistine is going to meet the same fate."

"All right," said Saul. "Go. Take my armor, and may God be with you."

A pair of soldiers helped David on with Saul's armor. The armor was so big and heavy that David took one step and fell over.

"Forget it," David said. "I can't walk, let alone fight, with this on me."

David peeled the armor off and stood in his tunic. He looked across the valley at Goliath. Fighting the giant in hand-to-hand combat would be suicide, he told himself. Then David remembered his sling. David picked up five smooth stones from the creek and put them in his bag. With his staff in hand, he walked past the Israelite front line.

"If I can stay out of his javelin range, I'll have a chance," he said to himself. "If only I had practiced more with Elhanon."

The Philistine saw David approach and spat in the dirt.

"I'm a dog that you send a boy with a stick! Damn you, boy! Damn you, Israelites! And damn your impotent god! Come here, boy, so I can feed your carcass to the vultures."

David froze for a moment, wondering if he had made a big mistake by being too brash. But it's too late now, he told himself. I've gone too far.

The spirit of God strengthened him and he said, "You come at me with a sword, javelin, and spear. I come with Adonai, the God of Israel. I'm going to kill you, cut off your head, and feed *your* carcass to the vultures. And then everybody will know that God saves not with sword and spear."

Goliath roared, "You little queer!" and lurched toward David. David ran toward the giant, took a stone from his bag, and slung it. The stone grazed Goliath's left shoulder. Goliath sensed the danger from a well-aimed stone and rushed David. David's hand froze in his bag. He wasn't going to have time to get off a second shot before Goliath would be on him. David stood rooted to the ground.

"This can't be happening," he told himself as the ground shook from Goliath's gait.

As David tensed himself preparing for the fatal blow, a rock whizzed by his ear and struck the giant in the gut. Goliath stopped suddenly, dropped his javelin, and clutched his stomach.

"Son-of-a-bitch!" screamed the Philistine. "I'm gonna rip your head off with my bare hands."

But while Goliath ranted, David quickly dropped a stone into his sling and slung it. The rock landed deep into the giant's forehead. Goliath tottered before falling face first onto the ground. For a long moment not a sound was heard between the two armies; the only movement was the small cloud of dust raised by Goliath's fall settling back to the ground.

David perceived a slight movement of Goliath's hand and sprinted to him. He grabbed the giant's sword with both hands and yanked it from its sheath. With one swing he guillotined Goliath's head from his shoulders. David held up the severed head and showed it to the Israelites. It was then that David saw Elhanon pat his sling and smile.* David nodded and turned to show the Philistines their champion's head. The Philistines fled and Israel gave chase.

Jonathan ran to David and hugged him.

"You were incredible! No, absolutely fantastic! You killed Goliath! My God!"

Jonathan stared into David's eyes.

"I love you as much as I love myself," Jonathan said, and the two of them returned to the palace.

●　◁▷　●

The Philistines did not keep Goliath's word about becoming Israelite slaves. Rather, they continued raiding Israel. Saul sent

* Cf. II Samuel 21:19.

David and his men to fight them, and David successfully beat them back.

A group of women once greeted one of David's victories with:

> Saul has slain his thousands,
> and David, his ten thousands.

"What!" shouted Saul when he heard the song. "Is he going to usurp my throne?" Saul picked up his spear and threw it through David's chair.

Jonathan found David and cried, "Quick! An evil spirit has gripped the king!"

David grabbed his lyre and ran to the throne room. Saul was sweating profusely.

"God," Saul whispered to the ceiling. "Am I not your anointed? Am I not king?" His voice rose. "Why did you choose the boy over me?"

Saul picked up the sacred Torah scroll and shook it at the ceiling.

"Speak to me!"

For a long moment, Saul stood with the Torah lifted above his head. Then he slowly lowered the scroll and said, "Your written words are also false."

An oil lamp sat on a nearby table. Saul started to lower the Torah into the flame. Up until now, David had been still, but he could not bear watching God's book desecrated.

"Stay your hand, Your Majesty!" David called out. "Listen."
David strummed his lyre.

> The Lord is my shepherd;
> I lack nothing.
> God lets me lie in green pastures
> And leads me to still waters ...

Saul dropped the Torah, grabbed his spear, and threw it. David somersaulted out of the way as Jonathan screamed, "Father!" Saul took up his sword and charged. Jonathan grabbed Saul's arm, giving David time to scramble to his feet and race out the door.

That night David spoke to Jonathan.

"What is my crime, my guilt, that your father wants to kill me?"

"He thinks you're going to steal the throne from him and usurp me. But I don't want to be king. You'll be king, and I'll serve you."

"It doesn't matter what *you* want," David said. "*He* wants me dead. I've got to leave."

The men kissed and cried over each other.

The next morning as David was packing to leave, Saul knocked on David's door.

"David, are you in there?"

David grabbed his belongings and threw them out the window. He put one leg out when Saul said through the closed door, "Son, I come in peace. Truly. I come to speak of my daughter."

The night before, after hearing of the attempt on David's life, Saul's daughter, Michal, told her father that she loved David. Like most Israelite women, Michal had fallen for the fine-looking musician/warrior. By pouring her heart out to her father, she hoped to save David's life.

Saul listened to Michal and thought, "I will give her to him and lead David to his death through Philistine hands."

"Son," Saul said through the closed door. "I was wrong. You are my most loyal servant, and I would be honored if you would take my daughter Michal as your wife."

David quickly grasped the advantage of such a marriage and opened the door. David bowed before Saul and said, "I would be honored to marry your daughter. But I am just the poor son of a shepherd. To become the son-in-law of a king is no small matter."

"Rise, my son," said Saul. "As always, you speak with wisdom beyond your years. You are wondering about the bride price. It is nothing. I desire nothing beyond the foreskins of one hundred Philistines."

David's eyes narrowed for a brief moment as he scrutinized the king. A wry smile appeared on Saul's face.

"It shall be done."

That night Jonathan tried to talk David out of the arrangement.

"Don't you see what he's up to? He gave you an impossible task in order to kill you! Don't you see?" Jonathan paused to let the words sink in and then added, "And you don't love Michal, right?"

"Adonai is the stronghold of my life," David said, taking Jonathan's hand. "When the Philistines attack me, it will be they who will stumble and fall."

And David was right. The spirit of God flowing through David combined with his bravery, his battle tactics, and his men's willingness to follow him anywhere created a fighting force that felled Philistines as easily as a lumberjack fells trees.

Soon David returned and counted out *two* hundred Philistine foreskins to Saul. Saul gave Michal to David, and the king grew more afraid of and more determined to kill his new son-in-law.

Saul came up with a new plan. He called in Jonathan.

"Son, I know that you are fond of David. But listen, unless you kill him, he shall become king over you."

"Father, how can I kill your most trusted servant? David saved Israel by killing Goliath, and he's your best commander against the Philistines. Israel needs David. I can't kill him."

"Stupid child!" Saul ranted. "You're my worst enemy."

Jonathan stormed out of the room.

A while later, Saul came up with another plan. He sent a pair of men to David's home to kill him. Michal learned of the plot.

"David," she said as they lay in bed. "Do you love me?"

"Do I love you? I'm the luckiest man in the world to have you for my wife."

"But do you love me?"

"Didn't I risk my life to gain your father's bride price?"

Satisfied, Michal stroked David's curly hair.

"Father wants to kill you."

David sighed. "That's not exactly news."

"Two assassins are waiting for you outside our front door."

"What?"

"Shhh, not so loud. I have a plan, my love. Escape out the window. I'll put the house idol in the bed and pretend you're here."

"You would defy your father for me?"

"I would defy God for you. I love you. Go."

So David climbed out the window and escaped.

In the morning, the assassins sent a message that Saul requested David. Michal told them that David was sick and brought them to the bedroom doorway. Earlier she had put the idol in the bed and placed a net of goat hair on its head.

"He's sleeping," she whispered to the men. "Tell the king he will come as soon as he is well."

The men returned to Saul and told him that since David was ill, they did not kill him.

The king raged. "I don't care if he's at death's doorstep or feeling well enough to jump through a window! Drag him out of bed and cut off his damn head!"

The men returned to David's house, burst into his bedroom with swords drawn, and found the idol.

Saul raged against Michal.

"Why did you trick me and let my enemy get away, you whore!"

"Because David told me, 'Help me get away or I'll kill you.'"

"Stupid child!" Saul ranted. "You're my worst enemy."

Michal stormed out of the room.

●　●　●

David escaped with only his sandals and tunic. He came to the priest Ahimelech and begged for bread, a sword, and a change of clothing. He then crossed the border and, with his simple clothes, tried to hide his identity. He sought refuge with the Philistine king Achish. Achish's counselors, however, recognized David and told the king, "That's David, the Israelite warrior who's been a thorn in our side. We must kill him."

Two guards escorted David to King Achish's palace. One guard smiled at David. The other sang, "Saul has slain his thousands; David, his ten thousands."

David quickly calculated the worth of his life now that he had been recognized. He quickened his gait, threw off the hands of the guards, and screamed, "I am the god of the earth! Bow down to me! Wooooh! Wooooh!" David fell to the ground, picked up two handfuls of dirt and threw them into the air screeching, "Blessed is me! God of earth! Wooooh! Wooooh!"

Saliva ran down David's beard and he scratched marks on Achish's gate with his fingernails.

"Hear my prayer! Pray! Wooooh!"

"Why are you bringing me this lunatic?" said Achish, glaring at his counselors. "Am I not already surrounded by madmen?"

The counselors quickly escorted David out of the palace.

●　●　●

David knew that Saul would come after him, so he gathered four hundred men who owed debts to or were guilty of crimes against Saul. David formed this riffraff into a small army.

Saul took three thousand men to find David. First he came to Ahimelech. When he heard that Ahimelech had helped David escape, Saul put him and his eighty-five priests to death. Then he followed David's trail to the desert oasis of En-gedi. David and his men were hiding in a large cave, while Saul's men swarmed over the rocks of En-gedi.

"Shhh, someone approaches," David whispered. A single man appeared at the cave's entrance—Saul. He entered the cave to rest. When Saul lay down, David's men hissed, "Let's kill him!"

David crept up to Saul, took out his knife, and silently cut the corner of Saul's cloak. Minutes later, Saul arose and left the cave.

David followed Saul out of the cave and called, "My lord king!"

The bewildered Saul turned and saw David prostrate on the ground.

"Why do you think I want to harm you," David began. "You can see for yourself that God delivered you into my hands right now in the cave, but I showed you pity, for you are God's anointed. Please, look at the corner of your cloak in my hand. I didn't kill you. I have never wronged you and am your trustworthy servant. Yet, you want to take my life."

Saul cried, "You are right, my son David. I now know that you will become king instead of Jonathan. Swear to me that you won't harm him."

"I swear it."

Saul and his men went home. David and his men went up to their stronghold.

Feeding an army now six hundred strong was not easy. Sometimes David raided Philistine towns for supplies. Sometimes the residents of areas protected by David fed them. One day David and his men were in Carmel, an area that they had kept safe from the Philistines. A wealthy but miserly man named Nabal lived there with his beautiful wife, Abigail.

Messengers from David came to Nabal and asked for food.

Nabal answered, "Who is this David that I should take the bread, water, and meat that I give to my own people, and give to men who come from I don't know where? Maybe you're all just a bunch of escaped slaves, eh? You dress like it."

"Nobody spurns David," said David, when his messengers came back empty-handed. "I protected his shepherds and his possessions, and now he pays me back evil for good. By nightfall his men will all be dead."

David and his men girded on their swords and started up the road.

When Abigail heard what her husband had done, she quickly threw together two hundred bread loaves, two barrels of wine, and five dressed sheep. She mounted a donkey and rode to David.

Abigail threw herself at David's feet and said, "My lord, please pay no attention to Nabal's words. He is a boor. Take these gifts and spare us. Please, my lord, I beg you."

Abigail remained head bowed to the ground.

"She is a beautiful woman, is she not?" David remarked to his right-hand man, Joab.

He nodded. "Also brave."

"And has good sense," added Joab's nephew, Abishai.

"Rise, good woman," commanded David. "You are to be praised. Your actions kept us from killing Nabal and his men. You are free to go home."

Abigail rose and permitted herself to gaze into the face of David. She instantly fell in love with him. As for David, he was struck by Abigail and desired her. He was tempted to break his word and kill Nabal in order to take her for a wife, since Saul had given Michal, David's wife, to another man when David was on the run. But as things worked out, David got his way without lifting a finger. Nabal died of natural causes ten days later, and David wed Abigail.

"I take no credit for this," said God when Gabriella accused God of meddling in human affairs. "It was pure coincidence. Really. Trust Me."

* * *

Time passed and once again Saul gathered his army to hunt David. Once again David passed up the chance to kill Saul. This time David stole Saul's spear and water jug while the king was sleeping, surrounded by his men. And once again Saul apologized to David and returned home. This time, however, David realized that Saul would never leave him in peace, so David fled to the Philistines. He came to King Achish and explained his situation with Saul. Achish granted David the town of Ziklag on the condition that David would raid Israelite towns.

David agreed. He and his men settled in Ziklag, but they raided Philistine towns.

"When we raid, leave no man or woman alive," David commanded his men. "If Achish finds out what we're doing, he'll kill us."

Following one such raid, David sat quietly by himself. The spirit of God, which had been his constant companion since he was anointed, seemed harder to sense as of late. David picked up his lyre for the first time in weeks.

> O Lord, I set my hope on You;
> Teach me Your ways;
> Guide me in Your true way and teach me,

For You are God, my deliverer;
It is You I look to at all times.

David put down his lyre.

"What am I to do? Power only understands power. It doesn't care about compassion or righteousness. Innocence and guilt make no difference. Oh God, how I yearn for the days of my youth when I knew right was right and wrong was wrong. I need your guidance now."

A small voice came to David. "Compassion and righteousness matter. Right is still right, and wrong is still wrong. It is yourself that you need to examine."

"God is a true judge," David said to himself and resolved to heed God's words.

● ▬ ●

Because David was in Ziklag hiding from Saul, the Philistines decided it was time to crush Israel. The entire Philistine army advanced deep into Israel. Since David chose to remain out of the fight, the Philistines quickly routed Saul's army, chasing them up Mount Gilboa. Saul's soldiers fell and a spear ended Jonathan's life. Saul had no time to mourn the death of his first-born as archers besieged him. Two arrows struck him and he knew he was finished.

"Take your sword and run me through," he gasped to his arms-bearer.

The arms-bearer stood motionless. To kill God's anointed was unthinkable.

Saul stumbled to the arms-bearer and snatched his sword. Saul steadied himself, looked up to heaven, and cursed God before throwing himself upon the blade.

The Philistines thus took control of Israel.

A young Amalekite man ran to Ziklag and told David that Saul and Jonathan were dead.

"How do you know the king and the prince are dead?" David asked.

It was common knowledge that Saul wanted David dead. The man cleared his throat and said, "Saul was on Mount Gilboa and the Philistines were closing in. He said to me, 'Finish me off, for I am barely alive.' So I killed him, for I knew he was done for. Here are his crown and armlet."

The Amalekite stood before David waiting for his reward. Instead, David was livid. "How did you dare lift your hand to kill God's anointed?"

David called one of his personal guards and commanded him to kill the man. David then tore his clothing and cried over Saul and Jonathan.

> *Daughters of Israel*
> *Weep over Saul*
> *Who clothed you in crimson*
> *Who decked your robes in jewels and gold.*
> *I grieve for you my brother Jonathan.*
> *You were most dear to me.*
> *Precious was your love to me,*
> *More than the love of women.*

With Saul's death, David became the king of Judah, and blood poured like winter rain in the land. Saul's surviving son, Ish-bosheth, crowned himself king of Israel and a civil war ensued. David prevailed and united Judah and Israel into one nation. But once the Philistines learned that David had become king of a united Israel, they attacked. This time the armies of Israel decisively defeated the Philistines.

"From the moment Samuel ended my peaceful shepherd's life with his anointing oil, I have only known war," David prayed to God. "Now that the Philistines are defeated and Israel is united, Your nation is at peace. Is now the time to bring the Ark of God to Jerusalem, the City of Peace?"

"Yes," said God. "Now is a good time, because with humans, peace isn't permanent like a rock; it's a rainbow—beautiful, but fleeting. Bring the Ark while you can."

David immediately brought the Ark to Jerusalem. At the gates of the city, David spoke to the Israelites.

"My people, today is the happiest day of my life. We have finally fulfilled the promise made to our ancestors and have become a single, united nation of God's chosen people. Through our many battles, all of us have suffered great pain and have lost loved ones; yet, with God on our side, we have succeeded. The nation Israel lives and will be a light unto the nations. Today the Ark of God will move to its permanent home in our great city. Let the procession begin!"

David strummed his lyre and sang.

I will praise You, Adonai, with all my heart
I will tell about all Your wonders.
I will be happy and rejoice in You,
I will sing Your name, O Most High

On this day, however, singing was not enough for David. He handed off his lyre and stripped down to his linen ephod. Then he danced and whirled with all of his might. Israel clapped and screamed in delight, God smiled at the sight, but Michal, David's first wife who was returned to him after the death of Saul, was unhappy with her husband.

"You did yourself great honor today, exposing yourself to the slave girls as if you were some lowlife scum."

"I danced before God who chose me over your father and

family to be king. And I will dance again before Adonai and dishonor myself even more in your eyes; but I will be honored among the slave girls that you speak of."

Michal shook with fury and stormed out of the room, never again to share her bed with David, and she died childless.

● ● ●

True to God's prediction, the peace between Israel and her coastal neighbor did not last long. Besides fighting the Philistines, David battled the Moabites, the Arameans, the Edomites, and the Ammonites. God brought David victory wherever he went, and Israel became the most powerful nation in its corner of the world.

Israel had just defeated Ammon and was besieging the city of Rabbah. For this battle, David sent Joab to lead the Israelite army, while he remained in Jerusalem. Late one afternoon, David rose from his couch and strolled along the palace roof. He was admiring the buildings of his beautiful city when his eyes alighted on a sight that made him stop and stare—a beautiful woman bathing. Though David had many wives and numerous concubines, he had never seen such a beauty, and he immediately sent for her.

One month later, the woman, Bathsheba, sent a message to David that she was pregnant. Unfortunately for David, Bathsheba was a married woman, married to Uriah, a general who was off fighting Rabbah.

David immediately sent for Uriah to return to Jerusalem to give report on the battle. After hearing the report, David told Uriah to go home to his wife and take a rest from fighting. Unfortunately for David, Uriah refused to sleep at home while his soldiers were at war. David tried talking Uriah into going home and even got him drunk, but Uriah would not budge.

"I've no choice," David said, and he sent Uriah back to the battle with a note for Joab. The note instructed Joab to assign Uriah to a place where he was certain to be killed.

"Good," said David upon hearing the news of Uriah's death. "That could have been a sticky situation."

"Bad," said God to Gabriella. "My boy has lost his moral compass. Rather than shepherding my flock, he is taking the choice ewes for himself."

So God sent the prophet Nathan to chastise David.

Nathan said to David, "There once were two men—one rich, the other poor. The rich man had very large flocks and herds, but the poor man had only one ewe. One day, a traveler came to the rich man, but the rich man didn't want to take from his own flocks to serve a meal to the traveler, so he took the poor man's lamb and served it."

David cried, "Who is this man? He deserves to die! He shall pay for the lamb four times over!"

"The man is you. You don't have enough women that you had to spurn God by taking Uriah's wife and having him killed?"

David bowed his head. "I stand guilty before Adonai."

"God will forgive your sin; you will not die. However, your unborn son will."

David prayed to God.

> God, You know my crime;
> My sins are not hidden from You.
> I am a worm, less than a man.
> Answer me, Adonai, for Your compassion is good.
> Turn Your abundant mercy toward me.
> Do not hide Your face for I'm in trouble.
> Answer me quickly.

But God did not answer David, and the baby died.
David looked to heaven.

> My God, my God
> Why have You abandoned me?

The heavens were silent.

• ⬭ •

Throughout his long reign, David sired many children, but it was an open question whether or not his children gave him comfort. One son raped one of his daughters. All the sons fought among themselves as to who would become king after David. And one son, Absalom, started an armed rebellion to overthrow his father.

In addition to his children, David had other problems as well. Another civil war between Israel and Judah broke out, and the Philistines invaded Israel again. David went out to lead Israel against the invaders, but the days of the young king bravely leading his troops in battle were long gone. He was a tired old man, and at one point his soldiers needed to rescue him in the midst of a fight.

"With all due respect, Your Majesty," said one of his generals gingerly, "I think you should no longer come out to battle."

• ⬭ •

Despite it all, David held the kingdom of Israel together. After forty years as monarch, David grew old, tired, and cold. His counselors brought him the kingdom's most beautiful girl to sleep by his side, but even her heat could not warm David. As David lay enfeebled in bed, his son Adonijah declared himself king without a word to David. David, however, had earlier promised the throne to Solomon, the second child he had with Bathsheba. As his last kingly act, David instructed that Solomon be anointed king.

After giving up the throne, David visited Jonathan's grave.

"I envy you, my friend," David said. "To die before your world and your body unravels is a great gift. It is true that I have had an enviable life: Power, fame, and luxury were fruits I greatly enjoyed. Yet, I had to fight every step of the way, and even now with the hand of death on my shoulder, I still cannot find peace.

"Perhaps you may think, 'Ah, but the years must have brought wisdom to David.' Don't be so sure. The world seemed much clearer when I was young. The wisdom I once had has been muddled by the years. I'm not sure I can even distinguish right from wrong, or good from evil. Yet, as my life draws to a close, I look back to see that I have been blessed with one constant that has strengthened and guided me since the days of my youth."

David took up his oldest possession, his lyre, and strummed one last time:

> Adonai, You are my lamp;
> O God, You give light to my darkness.
> The way of God is pure;
> Adonai's word is perfect;
> You have given me Your shield of protection
> And have made me great.
> Adonai lives! Blessed is my rock.

That evening, David died.

● ◍ ◉

"Imperfect as he was, he was good," God said to Gabriella.

Gabriella, usually loquacious regarding the foibles of God's human experiment, silently nodded.

About the Author

Matt Biers-Ariel, a popular teacher and storyteller, is author of *The Seven Species* and *Solomon and the Trees* as well as co-author of *Spirit in Nature*. He taught biblical and rabbinic texts for fifteen years. He now teaches high school English and lives in California with his wife and two sons.

About SKYLIGHT PATHS Publishing

SkyLight Paths Publishing is creating a place where people of different spiritual traditions come together for challenge and inspiration, a place where we can help each other understand the mystery that lies at the heart of our existence.

Through spirituality, our religious beliefs are increasingly becoming a part of our lives—rather than *apart* from our lives. While many of us may be more interested than ever in spiritual growth, we may be less firmly planted in traditional religion. Yet, we do want to deepen our relationship to the sacred, to learn from our own as well as from other faith traditions, and to practice in new ways.

SkyLight Paths sees both believers and seekers as a community that increasingly transcends traditional boundaries of religion and denomination—people wanting to learn from each other, *walking together, finding the way.*

We at SkyLight Paths take great care to produce beautiful books that present meaningful spiritual content in a form that reflects the art of making high quality books. Therefore, we want to acknowledge those who contributed to the production of this book.

Other Interesting Books—Spirituality

Journeys of Simplicity: *Traveling Light with Thomas Merton, Bashō, Edward Abbey, Annie Dillard & Others*
by *Philip Harnden*

There is a more graceful way of traveling through life. Offers vignettes of forty "travelers" and the few ordinary things they carried with them—from place to place, from day to day, from birth to death. What Thoreau took to Walden Pond. What Thomas Merton packed for his final trip to Asia. What Annie Dillard keeps in her writing tent. What an impoverished cook served M. F. K. Fisher for dinner. Much more. "'How much should I carry with me?' is the quintessential question for any journey, especially the journey of life. Herein you'll find sage, sly, wonderfully subversive advice." —Bill McKibben, author of *The End of Nature* and *Enough*

5 x 7¼, 128 pp, HC, ISBN 1-893361-76-4 **$16.95**

The Alphabet of Paradise: *An A–Z of Spirituality for Everyday Life*
by *Howard Cooper*

Howard Cooper takes us on a journey of discovery—into ourselves and into the past—to find the signposts that can help us live more meaningful lives. In twenty-six engaging chapters—from A to Z—Cooper spiritually illuminates the subjects of daily life, using an ancient Jewish mystical method of interpretation that reveals both the literal and more allusive meanings of each. Topics include: Awe, Bodies, Creativity, Dreams, Emotions, Sports, and more.
"An extraordinary book." —Karen Armstrong

5 x 7¾, 224 pp, Quality PB, ISBN 1-893361-80-2 **$16.95**

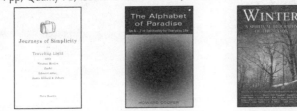

Winter: *A Spiritual Biography of the Season*
Edited by *Gary Schmidt* and *Susan M. Felch*; Illustrations by *Barry Moser*

Explore how the dormancy of winter can be a time of spiritual preparation and transformation. Includes selections by Will Campbell, Rachel Carson, Annie Dillard, Donald Hall, Ron Hansen, Jane Kenyon, Jamaica Kincaid, Barry Lopez, Kathleen Norris, John Updike, E. B. White, and many others. "This outstanding anthology features top-flight nature and spirituality writers on the fierce, inexorable season of winter.... Remarkably lively and warm, despite the icy subject." —★*Publishers Weekly* Starred Review

6 x 9, 288 pp, 6 b/w illus., Deluxe PB w/flaps, ISBN 1-893361-92-6 **$18.95**
HC, ISBN 1-893361-53-5 **$21.95**

Or phone, fax, mail or e-mail to: SKYLIGHT PATHS Publishing
Sunset Farm Offices, Route 4 • P.O. Box 237 • Woodstock, Vermont 05091
Tel: (802) 457-4000 • Fax: (802) 457-4004 • www.skylightpaths.com

Credit card orders: (800) 962-4544 (8:30AM–5:30PM ET Monday–Friday)
Generous discounts on quantity orders. SATISFACTION GUARANTEED. Prices subject to change.